Odd Girl In

❋

Also by Jo Whittemore:

Front Page Face-Off

Odd Girl In

Jo Whittemore

ALADDIN M!X
NEW YORK   LONDON   TORONTO   SYDNEY

This book is a work of fiction. Any references to historical events, real people, or real locales are used fictitiously. Other names, characters, places, and incidents are the product of the author's imagination, and any resemblance to actual events or locales or persons, living or dead, is entirely coincidental.

ALADDIN M!X

Simon & Schuster Children's Publishing Division

1230 Avenue of the Americas, New York, NY 10020

First Aladdin M!X edition March 2011

Copyright © 2011 by Jo Whittemore

For information about special discounts for bulk purchases, please contact Simon & Schuster Special Sales at 1-866-506-1949 or business@simonandschuster.com.

The Simon & Schuster Speakers Bureau can bring authors to your live event. For more information or to book an event contact the Simon & Schuster Speakers Bureau at 1-866-248-3049 or visit our website at www.simonspeakers.com.

Designed by Ann Zeak

The text of this book was set in Garamond.

Manufactured in the United States of America 0211 OFF

10 9 8 7 6 5 4 3 2 1

Library of Congress Control Number 2010933797

ISBN 978-1-4424-1284-2

ISBN 978-1-4424-1285-9 (eBook)

For my Sweethearts—Jessica and Tricia

Acknowledgments

Always for God, family, friends, and fans.

For my editor, Alyson Heller, who shares my sense of humor, twisted as it may be.

For my agent, Jenn Laughran, who always has the right words.

For my critique partner, Cheryl Peevyhouse, who knows my mind.

For Pat Bly, who throws me floaties, chocolates . . . whatever it takes.

For Julie Terry, who shares stories of book love and also, my passion for shoes.

For the Montgomery High School Class of '95, my support squad.

For the fabulous folks on the YANovelists listserv, who dispense ideas and advice so willingly.

And for my SCBWI crew, who span the globe and laugh at all the right places in my stories.

Love

Chapter 1 ❊

All I did was put a flaming bag of dog poop on Mr. McGuire's porch.

He was *supposed* to stomp it out and get dog doo on his shoes, then maybe wave a wrinkly fist and yell Old People Gibberish. I'd seen it in the movies a hundred times.

Well, apparently Mr. McGuire hadn't been to the movies in a while. Instead of stomping, he attacked the fire with his newspaper. But since he was old and slow, he barely tapped the bag and the *newspaper* caught on fire.

"Oh, crumb," he muttered.

Mr. McGuire waved the paper around, but of course that only made the fire spread faster, until the flames were bigger than his head. When I saw smoke coming from the wispy ends of his comb-over, I couldn't take it anymore.

I jumped up from my hiding spot and raced across the lawn. Once I reached Mr. McGuire, I knocked the paper out of his hand and patted the sparks out of his hair.

"There," I said, panting and stomping on the bag. "Fire's out."

Unfortunately, I kind of overlooked the burning newspaper that had landed on his porch sofa.

And that was how I discovered the flammability of wicker.

By the time I could act, the foam cushions on the sofa were already a charred black mass, and the frame was a miniature bonfire.

"Water, Alexis!" Mr. McGuire yelled at me. "We need water!"

I ran next door to my house and grabbed the garden hose. A few minutes later, the fire was gone, along with half of Mr. McGuire's porch sofa. I couldn't help feeling partly to blame. I also couldn't think of a way to fix the situation.

Finally, I said, "Hey, at least your house wasn't touched. That's lucky."

"Lucky?" Mr. McGuire growled. "I lost a sofa *and* my newspaper! Before I'd even finished the crossword!"

"You can have *our* paper," I offered. "My dad only likes the Jumble and he . . ." I trailed off when I realized Mr. McGuire was giving me the evil eye.

"Alexisss." He hissed my name, pointing a gnarled finger. "*You* did this!"

"Um . . ." I started to back away, but Mr. McGuire gripped my arm.

"This is the last straw!" He shuffled toward my house, pulling me along while I tried to explain.

"It wasn't personal," I said. "You're just the closest house, and I didn't want to carry a bag of dog logs down the street!"

Ignoring my explanations, he gave the bottom of our front door a swift kick. Then he howled in pain and glared at me. "*Now* look at what you've done! I broke my toe!"

My eyes widened. "But you just—"

The door opened and Dad appeared, towering over both of us. "Mr. McGuire." He frowned when he saw me. "Alex, what's going on?"

Mr. McGuire pushed his way in front of me. "Your daughter broke my toe and tried to light me on fire. That's what's going on, Professor Evins!"

To his credit, Dad merely frowned. "I'm sorry. How exactly did this happen?" He wrinkled his nose. "And *what* is that smell?"

"Oh! Sorry." I stepped off the porch and dragged the bottoms of my shoes over the grass. "It was a Flaming #2. Parker bet I couldn't leave one on someone's doorstep."

Dad groaned and called over his shoulder, "Parker! Get downstairs now! And bring Nick!" He smiled at Mr. McGuire. "Twins: If one's involved, the other can't be far behind."

"Neither can their sister." Mr. McGuire glowered at me. "She lit my sofa on fire!"

Dad held up a hand. "Wait. . . . I thought she tried to light *you* on fire."

"She *did*." Mr. McGuire leaned toward Dad conspiratorially. "And when she couldn't succeed, she went after my furniture!"

I grabbed Dad's arm. "It was totally an accident. I swear."

I explained what happened, and Dad walked out onto our porch to see for himself. It only took one glance at Mr. McGuire's sofa skeleton for Dad's eyebrows to raise into his hairline.

"That sofa cost six hundred dollars," said Mr. McGuire. "I expect you to pay for it."

Dad made a choking sound in the back of his throat and nodded. "That's . . . understandable. I'll have a check for you tomorrow."

Mr. McGuire shook his head. "Not good enough! I *demand* you send your rotten kids to one of those child labor camps. Or a sweatshop." He sneered at me. "How would you like to make sneakers for a dime an hour?"

I looked up at Dad, who gave the slightest shake of his head. "Mr. McGuire, the punishment will fit the crime. I can assure you. And I want to apologize for what happened, as do my children." He turned to Nick and Parker, who had been staring daggers at me from the staircase. "*All* of them."

My brothers were high school freshmen and *hated* being called children, but the tone in Dad's voice meant there was no arguing.

"Sorry, Mr. McGuire," said Nick.

"We apologize," added Parker.

Dad nodded at me, and I sighed. "I'm sorry too."

Mr. McGuire's mouth moved for a moment, like he wanted to say something else, but he just grunted and walked away.

"Have my money tomorrow!" he finally managed.

We watched him totter up his sidewalk, and I turned to Dad with a grateful smile.

He didn't smile back.

"My office. *Now*," he said, including my brothers in his ominous gaze.

Bowing my head, I followed him through the house. Nick and Parker fell into step behind us, and Parker pushed me so that I almost stumbled into Dad.

"Nice going, pyromaniac," he said. "Can't you follow simple instructions?"

"I don't know." I glared at him. "Tell me to push you off the roof and let's see what happens."

"Both of you shut up before you get us in trouble." Nick grabbed Parker and me by our necks and squeezed. Since I was a scrawny twelve-year-old girl, I flinched and went quiet. Since Parker was *built* like a scrawny twelve-year-old girl, he did the same.

"I'm afraid you're far past trouble," said Dad.

He sat at his desk and gestured for the three of us to sit in the two chairs on the opposite side. Nick automatically got one of the seats because he was bigger and stronger, while Parker and I got into a slap/push/pinch fight for the other one.

"I'm older than you. I get to sit," said Parker.

"There's not enough room on that chair for you and your hair," I said.

My brothers and I all have blue eyes and dark hair, but Parker has dark, bushy "genius" hair, which he claimed separated him and Albert Einstein from the "regular" smart people. When he wasn't tangled up in schoolwork, he was tangled up in the shaggy madness on his shoulders.

It took a couple of minutes for us to realize that Dad was watching us silently, and Nick had his head buried in his hands. Even though I didn't want to, I let Parker have the chair and sat against the bookcase.

Dad cleared his throat. "That behavior you just displayed is part of our problem. The three of you should be working together, not constantly bickering."

"But *all* brothers and sisters fight," said Nick. "It's on television and in the movies. It's a normal part of life. Brothers even fought against each other in wars!"

Parker might have been the smarter twin, but Nick was usually the voice of reason. Unfortunately, Dad wasn't interested.

"And did all these *other* siblings earn cruel nicknames from the neighbors?" he asked.

"Hey, only Mr. McGuire calls us the Evil Evins," I spoke up from the floor.

"And technically, it should be Evinses," said Parker. "Because the plural, uh, doesn't really matter." He shrank back as Dad got out of his chair and paced around us.

"Alex," Dad said without looking at me. "Why on *earth* did you pull a dangerous stunt like that?"

"Nick and Parker made me do it," I said. As soon as the words were out, I regretted them.

Dad spun to face me. "I'm sorry. You said your brothers *made* you do this?"

Dad was a philosophy professor at the university and the world's biggest supporter of free will (the idea that people always have a choice). He even had T-shirts made for his students with FREE WILL TO GOOD HOME. printed on them.

"They said that if I didn't drop the Flaming #2, I was just a little girl," I said. "I had to defend my honor."

"Alex," said Dad in a low voice, "you *are* a little girl. And *you* two"—he pointed at my brothers—"are bad influences. I hold you just as responsible for what happened tonight."

My brothers shouted in protest at the same time I argued, "I am *not* a little girl! I'm in junior high!"

"Quiet!" bellowed Dad.

It's pointless to argue when you're up against those lungs.

"I've been thinking about this for a while now," he said. We watched him pull a handful of junk out of his pocket before he found a wadded-up tissue to wipe his reading glasses with. Then he had to search for *those*.

Dad was endlessly disorganized. If it wasn't for our housekeeper, his office would be an explosion of papers, magazines, and really heavy books. But he assured us that his external chaos was the perfect balance to his incredibly focused mind. I believed him most of the time, except when he called me Parker.

We found the glasses in his raincoat pocket, and Dad rubbed them clean before slipping them on.

"Every week the three of you seem to be in some new sort of trouble."

"Well, Nick and Parker——," I started, but Dad cut me off.

"Do not control you. They have, however, been unusually strong influences in your life. Do you know why?"

I knew why, but I couldn't tell Dad.

Because it involved Mom.

Both my parents had taught at the same university. That's where they'd met, Dad falling for Mom way before *she* noticed *him*. She was always so wrapped up in research, Dad joked about juggling knives just to get her attention. It probably should have been a sign, but he didn't realize it.

My brothers and I had awkward childhoods. Mom would give us IOUs for family time and hire strangers to run our birthday parties. Then, when I was seven, Mom received a grant from the National Science Foundation and headed to Bermuda for six months. Her research was so successful that the time stretched into a year, and then it became indefinite. She sent us a note, along with a batch of birthday and Christmas checks, saying she couldn't leave her research to lesser minds and that we'd be better off.

It might have been easy for her, but the rest of us were devastated. Nick gave up on his schoolwork entirely; Parker wouldn't do anything *but* schoolwork; I refused to eat, preferring to cry and swivel in Mom's old chair.

Until one night, when I caught Dad doing the same thing.

That was when I knew I needed to be tough . . . for myself, my dad, *and* my brothers. It made things easier if I was just one of the guys and not a small reminder of Mom.

So when Dad said, "Do you know why?" I shook my head and simply asked, "Why?"

"Because you don't have enough discipline." He turned to my brothers. "None of you do."

"Maybe we would if *you* were around more," grumbled Parker.

That was another thing: When Mom left, Dad picked up her old habits, hiding in his office and burying himself deep in philosophical books. Of course, my brothers and I weren't worried about *him* leaving. Dad could never even find his socks for one day, let alone pack for a six-month expedition. Still, Parker had a point.

Dad's face turned slightly pink and he wandered back to his desk. "Unfortunately, someone has to feed this family and pay for barbecued couches."

Nick, always the quickest of us to stop trouble, pulled his chair closer to Dad's desk. "We know you're busy, but when we're on our own something bad is bound to happen."

Dad stared at his desk for a moment before looking up.

"Well, it's time to put a stop to that. I want each of you to reach your full potential." He opened his desk drawer and pulled out a stack of green pamphlets, handing them to Nick. "And this is the best way."

I frowned at the pamphlet Nick gave me, already dreading what was inside. The cover featured a smiling gold star in a blue T-shirt, one of my biggest pet peeves. It was my firm belief that *nothing* but a person should ever wear clothing. A star in a T-shirt made as much sense as a poodle in a prom dress.

Above the obnoxious star appeared the word CHAMPS! in bright, bold letters. I opened my pamphlet to the next page and was instantly struck by the image of six girls in a human pyramid.

"Cheerleading?!" I cried. "You think my full potential is a . . . a set of pom-poms and a high kick?"

I turned to my brothers, who looked just as horrified.

"No, no, no." Nick shook his head with enough force to make *me* dizzy. "I can't be a cheerleader *and* date them! Plus, I don't have enough rhythm for all the clapping!"

"And cheerleading instantly reduces your IQ one hundred points," said Parker. "*I'd* still be okay, but Nick and Alex—"

"It's *not* cheerleading." Dad ran his fingers through his hair. "Would any of you like to actually *read* the pamphlet before you jump to conclusions?"

So we did. I sat on the edge of Dad's desk and skimmed the text.

"Welcome to *Champs*!" I read aloud, making sure to give the last word plenty of sarcastic energy. "The best investment you'll *ever* make for your child."

"I thought college was the best investment," interrupted Parker. He paled to the color of cafeteria tuna and looked at Dad. "Are you sending us to cheerleading camp instead of college?"

Dad groaned and rubbed his temples. "For the last time, this has nothing to do with cheerleading." He gestured vaguely in my direction. "Alex, keep reading."

"Our life-skills course is designed to turn your bright, shining child into a bright, shining star. In just four short weeks—" I interrupted myself this time. "Four weeks?! This torture is going to last a month?"

"It won't be torture," said Dad, taking my pamphlet and turning the page. "Look at all the fun activities, like . . . Adventures in Organization. Adventure, Alex!" He waggled his fingers in front of me, trying to make it exciting.

I rolled my eyes. "Dad, anything sounds fun if you put it *that* way." I waggled my fingers like he had. "A magical trip to the dentist!"

Parker snorted. "She's right . . . for once."

"Yeah," said Nick. "There's no adventure in organization. I cleaned my locker on Friday, and I'm pretty sure nothing exciting happened."

Parker nudged him. "You found that dollar."

Nick brightened. "Oh yeah."

I shot both of them a dirty look, and Dad smiled. "There, you see? Being organized paid off . . . literally."

"But, Dad," said Parker, "I already have all these skills. I shouldn't have to go."

"Really?" Dad crossed his arms. "How long did you spend on your hair this morning?"

"I . . ." Parker leaned back, covering his hair protectively. "The same amount of time as always."

Dad raised an eyebrow. "Which is . . ."

"Forever." I couldn't help chiming in. "I can get dressed and eat breakfast before you're done."

"I can get dressed, eat, *and* brush my teeth," said Nick.

Parker glared at both of us, and Dad cleared his throat. "I think you could use a little more time management."

"And a little less hair gel," I added.

Parker lunged for me, but Dad pushed him back into his seat.

"The class is every Tuesday and Thursday, and you start this week," said Dad. "But it's not enough to just show up." He looked at each of us in turn, to make sure he had our full attention. "You have to *pass* the class. All of you."

13

Seeing the no-nonsense expression on Dad's face, Nick raised his hand. "I'm not sure—"

Dad stopped him with a motion. "All of you pass, or all of you fail. Like I said before, you need to learn to work together."

"What happens if we fail?" asked Parker.

Dad sighed and leaned against his desk. "You know, I'm not asking you to do the impossible," he said. "But if you can't get your acts together for even a few weeks . . ."

Nick, Parker, and I leaned forward anxiously.

"I'm pulling you from public school and enrolling you at St. Ignatius."

The collective gasp from my brothers and me nearly sucked all the oxygen out of the room.

"But they're really strict!" I said. "I'll never get out of the principal's office."

"And I'm starting on the JV football team this year," said Nick. "That's *big* for a freshman. St. Ignasty doesn't even *have* a team."

Dad didn't say anything, just waited expectantly for Parker's complaint.

"If I have to change schools, I'll lose Ashley," he said, shoulders sagging so much that I almost felt sorry for him. Between my two brothers, it was the annoyingly smart one who had the steady girlfriend. And she was alive . . . and human . . . and even pretty.

I turned toward Dad and gave him my most desperate, most pleading pout. "Please don't make us do this."

Dad pressed his fingertips together, a sign he was going into Prof Mode. "To quote the great Lao Tzu, 'A journey of a thousand miles begins with a single step.' This one," he nodded at the pamphlet, "is yours."

🌼 Chapter 2

O n Monday, when Nick and I went downstairs for breakfast, we found a folded sheet of
paper waiting on each of our plates. We looked
at Dad, who smiled pleasantly and sipped his coffee.

"Good morning," he said.

I lifted my plate, letting the paper slide off. "You know,
in some countries these flat discs are used to hold food."

Nick picked up the fallen page. "If we have your paperwork, does that mean the bacon's in a filing cabinet?"

"The bacon is on the stove, my hilarious children," Dad
said. "Those are life assessment surveys for Champs."

Nick unfolded the paper and I read over his shoulder.
It was divided into three sections: Physical, Intellectual,

and Social. Under each category were several questions.

"Why do we have to fill these out?" I asked.

"So your Champs coach can see where you need improvement," said Dad. "According to Ms. Success—"

I glanced up from the paper. *"Who?"*

Dad sighed, as if dreading repeating the words. "Ms. Success, your Champs coach."

I looked at Nick and the two of us burst out laughing.

"All right, that's enough," said Dad. "Anyway, Ms. . . ." He paused, seeing the gleefully expectant looks on our faces. *"That woman* says a balanced life has equal strength of body, mind, and spirit."

I read over the physical questions. "Is that why she wants to know if we can swim? Or is the class under-water?"

"Just put 'yes,'" Dad said, an edge to his voice. "I'm sure it's important for *some* reason."

Nick chewed on his lip while he scanned the paper. "These intellectual questions are hard."

Dad frowned. "Please don't say that."

"Why?" asked Nick. "You know my grades aren't great."

"Yes, but the test you're holding is your sister's."

"Oh." Nick grimaced and looked at the paper folded on his own plate. "Darn."

"I can help you," said Parker, sliding into a chair.

Nick, Dad, and I all looked at him in surprise, not used to seeing Parker until the second it was time to leave the house.

"You're down early," said Dad. "And you still did . . . whatever to your hair. Very impressive."

"What can I say? I have excellent time-management skills," Parker said with a smug grin, reaching for his own survey.

Nick leaned toward him and sniffed. "No, you just didn't shower."

Parker blushed but kept his eyes on the page. "I don't sweat so I don't need to bathe every day."

I gave Dad a disgusted look, and he placed a hand on Parker's shoulder. "You're *not* cutting corners where hygiene is concerned."

Parker sighed and got up. "I suppose I'll go flush the toilet too, then."

"Ugh." I shook my head. "What does Ashley *see* in him?" It was a fair question since, of my twin brothers, Nick was the cleaner, *saner* one.

"Be nice," said Dad, tweaking my nose. "Or you're going to get a low score on the social portion of your survey."

Looking over the questions, I realized that was going to happen no matter what:

18

List all the clubs you belong to.

List all of your social activities.

How many kids would consider you their friend?

How often do you hang out with your friends?

My answer to those questions was either zero, nothing, never, or none. I was quite possibly the most antisocial twelve-year-old on the planet. And I had dear old Mom to thank for that.

When I first started kindergarten, she had taught me to be independent and to not get too friendly with anyone. She didn't want other kids, or "obstacles" as she called them, to distract me from learning. Since I'd spent my playpen years watching Mom cradle a research book instead of *me*, it wasn't too much of a change. And if it made her smile that I could finger paint better than anyone, it was worth it.

But then she left a few years later, and I was stuck with zero social skills around kids who had already built friendships with one another. So it wasn't that kids hated me or that I hated them; we'd just never spent time together. And after Mom, I didn't really want to bond with anyone. Especially not with other girls.

I filled out the physical and intellectual portions of the survey and left the social part blank until I got to school.

Once there, I sat in the courtyard, wondering who my friends were and what I could list for a club or social activity.

I'd been in detention once with a few other kids, but that probably didn't count as a club. And going on field trips probably didn't count as a social activity, even if I did let Emily Gold sit with me on the bus and listened to her constant babbling.

Emily Gold. Now *there* was somebody who would have done even worse than me on the social portion of the survey. Like Parker, she was smart; and like Nick, she was athletic. She was the class princess who could ace anything while wearing a beauty pageant smile and a gold ribbon in her perfect ponytail. Naturally, almost everyone hated her.

But not to her face of course.

The bell rang and I headed for PE, tucking my survey into my pocket. Emily was already in the girls' locker room when I got there, smiling at her reflection in a bathroom mirror.

"Hello, Alexis," she said, catching my eye.

I'd given up long ago on getting her to call me Alex. She refused to believe I could use a boy's name and not automatically sprout a beard.

"Hi, Em," I said with a smile.

She cleared her throat. "It's *Emily*."

"It's Alex," I said, pointing to myself.

Emily turned from the mirror to face the real me. "I like Alexis better."

"Than Emily? Me too." I smiled again to show I was joking, but she just rolled her eyes.

"Are you going to Chloe's slumber party this weekend? I mean . . ." She glanced around nervously. "You *did* get invited, didn't you?"

Since I wasn't in a particular clique, I was seen as a safe bet for most social invites, but Emily wasn't wrong to ask. I'd turned down every girlie event since the start of the school year.

"Yes, I got invited," I said, opening my locker. "But I'm not going. The invitation mentioned nail polish and pillow fights. I'm pretty sure there's going to be giggling, too."

Emily frowned. "You do realize that's what *normal* girls our age do?"

"What's normal?" I shrugged and changed into my gym clothes. "I'm just not into that kind of thing. I'd rather shoot spitballs at the ceiling."

Emily wrinkled her nose. "Classy."

"Hey, I use fancy cocktail napkins," I told her. "*And* they're recycled, so I'm being eco-friendly."

"Whatever," said Emily. "I really think you should go to the party. You don't socialize enough, and that can be unhealthy."

21

I raised an eyebrow. "Well, thank you for your professional opinion, *doctor*." I rubbed my chin thoughtfully. "You know, since you're giving out advice, maybe you can answer something else."

A flicker of surprise crossed Emily's face, but she stood a little taller. "Of course, Alexis. What is it?"

Glancing around, I pointed at a spot on my wrist. "Does this mole look like a chocolate chip to you?"

"Ugh!" Emily straightened and stalked away.

"Because I thought it was at first," I said, following her onto the gym floor, "but it really hurt when I bit it."

That at least got her to stop talking. We joined the line for badminton, our sport of the month, if it could be called a sport. Only two people in our class were any good at it: Emily, of course, and Chloe Stroupe.

Chloe was the ultracompetitive type, the girl who joined any and every team that had a chance of winning a trophy. She even dressed like a boy once to score extra medals at a track meet. Normally she was a nice person, but if someone stood between her and glory, they wound up facedown with her sneaker marks on their back.

I was up first against Chloe, so I grabbed my favorite racket out of the bin. I could tell it was mine because one side was warped from where I'd banged it against the gym floor every time I missed the birdie. I might not have been good at badminton, but I didn't like to lose either. My mom had always stressed how important it was to be the best at whatever I did. She probably would have made a great Champs coach.

The gym teacher blew her whistle, and I walked to one side of the net while Chloe readied herself on the other. Someone tapped me on the shoulder, and I turned to see Emily twirling a shiny, dent-less racket that she'd brought from home.

"Keep your eye on the birdie," she said. "Every time you serve, you stare at your racket like you've never seen one before."

A couple of people in line snickered while I tried very hard for something less than a frown.

"Okay," I told Emily. "Thanks for the tip."

She smiled and walked off, ponytail bobbing behind her.

When I went for my first serve, I completely forgot her advice, and watched the racket as I hit the birdie straight into the net.

"Fault!" shouted Chloe. She was the wonderful kind of person who made a big deal out of every point she won and every fault made by her opponent.

"Keep your eyes on the birdie!" Emily yelled from her place in line. "*Be* the racket."

If I *had* been, I would have swatted *her* into the net, too.

23

Instead, I took a deep breath and picked up the birdie, tossing it to Chloe. Her serve cleared the net, and this time I kept my eye on the birdie. The minute it headed for my side of the net, I jumped up and slammed it back.

A few girls in line cheered.

"Fault!" shouted Chloe.

"What?!" I paused in the middle of a thank-you wave to the crowd. "That was *not* a fault. I hit it!"

"You're not allowed to reach over the other team's net!" called an annoying and all-too-familiar voice from the sidelines. "Next time you should——"

I threw down my racket (adding another dent to the collection) and stormed toward Emily. She at least had the common sense to stop talking and hide behind the teacher.

"Emily . . . shut . . . *up-puh*!" I said, turning the last word into a two-syllable one.

Now that she could see I wasn't going to stuff her racket down her throat, her know-it-all expression returned. "Your game needs work. I was trying——"

"This is *PE*!" I told her with an incredulous stare. "I'm not joining the Olympic team, and I *don't* need your help, Miss Know-It-All!"

Emily's lower lip quivered for a second, but she crossed her arms and stayed quiet.

"Alex," said the gym teacher, "let's unleash that anger on the birdie, okay?"

"Serve," I told Chloe, walking back across the court.

She then proceeded to beat me fifteen to ten. Her celebration move, playing her leg like an air guitar, was a fun reminder of my failure. But since it was the best I'd done so far, I dropped my racket in the bin without a word . . . until I felt someone tap me on the shoulder.

"Emily, I swear—" I spun to face her and took a step back when I realized it was someone else.

"You have to come to my party," said Chloe.

I squinted at her, confused. "Uh . . ."

She pushed her white blonde hair over her shoulder and glanced around before stepping closer. "Look, my mom made me invite Emily. *Nobody* likes her, but nobody will stand up to her if she gets annoying . . . except you."

"Why not?" I asked, looking past Chloe. "I'll bet if you yank Emily's ponytail, she'll go right down."

Chloe shook her head. "She's not a *physical* threat, but she's in good with all the teachers *and* her stepmom runs the PTA." She widened her eyes in fright. "All she has to do is say the word, and your schedule gets switched like *that.*" She snapped her fingers. "Any classes you have with your friends, gone."

I snorted. "First of all, I don't have any friends to worry about. Second of all, Emily is *not* that powerful."

"You know who else thought that?" Chloe's voice switched to a harsh whisper. "Dana Charles."

Dana was a year older than us and had mysteriously dropped out after the first week of school.

I narrowed my eyes. "Uh-huh. So you'd rather *I* get kicked out than you?"

Chloe shook her head. "You're not in any danger. Emily likes you for some strange reason."

"Thanks," I said flatly.

She clasped her hands in front of her. "Please, Alex. I'm begging you! I'll do whatever you want!"

I could overhear Emily complaining about the non-regulation birdies we used, and I was all set with a "no," but then I realized something.

Emily had, unfortunately, been right about my non-existent social circle. It was bound to come up in Champs and might keep me from passing the class . . . unless I added a few friendly outings.

"All right." I fixed Chloe with a steady gaze and spoke slowly. "I will help you on two conditions."

Chloe's eyes lit up, but she nodded seriously.

"Condition one," I held up a finger. "I don't have to sing alone *or* in a group to any musical number. And that includes lip-synching into a hairbrush."

She nodded. "I'll count you out of the dance routine too."

I didn't bother asking if she was serious. "Condition two: You provide me with earplugs, a laser pointer, a blank CD, and twenty dollars."

A flicker of confusion crossed Chloe's face. "Why?"

"Don't worry about that," I said. "I've dealt with Emily's kind before."

"Um, okay. Is that it?"

"Yep." I held out my hand so we could shake on it. "I'll see you in my polar bear pajamas."

Chloe grinned and squeezed my hand, hopping up and down. She giggled excitedly and sprinted away. When class ended, I managed to make it two steps into the locker room before Emily popped up directly in my path.

"Geez!" I jumped back. "Shouldn't you be wearing a ninja costume when you do that?"

Emily closed the gap between us. "That was really mean what you said earlier."

"What, calling you Miss Know-It-All?" I pushed past her and opened my locker. "I'm sorry I hurt your feelings, but you were kind of being a pain."

She shrugged. "It's okay. Since we're friends, I forgive you."

Fantastic. I now had *one* person who considered me a friend for my Champs survey. Not that the feeling was mutual. "Uh, thanks," I said, slipping into a bathroom stall to change. Normally, I wasn't so modest, but it was a chance to escape Emily.

Or so I thought.

Her feet appeared on the tile just outside my stall.

"We get graded on how we do out there, you know," she said from the other side of the door.

"I'm doing great," I said. "Don't worry."

"A 'B' is average," she corrected me.

With my shirt around my neck, I opened the stall door. "How do you know my grade?"

"I have access to *everyone's* grades," Emily said mysteriously. "If you want to do better, I can teach you."

"Thanks, but I'm all set." I closed the door.

"Think about it," she said. "We'll talk more tonight."

"Sorry," I said, slipping on my jeans. "I have plans."

"I *know.*" She made a scoffing sound. "They're with me and my stepmom."

I froze, one foot suspended in the air with an unlaced sneaker. "What?"

"You're in Champs, right?" asked Emily. "My stepmom teaches the class."

I sighed and sank down onto the toilet. "Of course she does."

"And I'm her assistant." Emily almost sounded proud.

"It's the first year she's trusted me with so much responsibility."

"Congratulations," I said. "If you'll excuse me, I think I'm going to be sick."

"You know what helps an upset stomach?" she asked. "If—"

I leaned back and flushed the toilet to drown her out. Maybe being a student at St. Ignatius wouldn't be so terrible.

❀ Chapter 3

If there was one thing I hated more than a poodle in a dress, it was *me* in a dress. But Dad insisted we look our best for the Champs evaluation.

"First impressions are very important," he said, helping Parker knot a tie. "Especially since you're joining the class a week late."

"We've already missed a week?" I asked, slipping into my sandals. "That's a lot of learning down the drain. Maybe we should just wait for the next round."

Dad smirked. "Nice try. Ms. Success will help you catch up on everything you missed."

"Ms. Success." Nick chuckled to himself.

Dad pointed a warning finger at him. "I don't want to hear a single 'ha,' 'hee,' or 'ho' out of you all night."

"Okay, okay," said Nick.

"Does everyone have their surveys ready?" Dad held out his hand, and we each passed ours over.

He studied them, wincing a little more with each new one he read.

"Hey!" I pulled at his arm. "We're right here. Save the disappointed face for when we're not around."

"No, it's not that," said Dad. "It's just . . . I should have helped you fill these out."

"What was wrong with mine?" asked Parker.

Dad gave him a look. "Do you really want me to say?"

Parker crossed his arms and lifted his chin. "I've got nothing to be ashamed of."

Dad cleared his throat. "The question was, 'How fast can you run?' You answered, 'As fast as my servants can carry me.'" Dad lowered the paper.

Nick and I laughed, and Parker did his best to play innocent. "Do you think Alfred Nobel did all his own running? He probably had a guy."

"You're so lame, dude," Nick told Parker.

"Nick," said Dad, "you said the capital of France was *F*." He pursed his lips. "It wasn't a spelling question."

I doubled over with laughter, and Parker slapped Nick on the back. "It's okay. You can get a job as one of my servants."

"And finally we come to Alex," said Dad, squeezing my shoulder. "For social groups, you can't count being a member at Sam's Club. Especially since it's my card."

By this point, we were all laughing, and even Dad couldn't resist a smile. "At least you'll all get flying colors in the humor category."

The Champs class was taught at the university where Dad worked, so he could drop us off on Tuesdays and Thursdays and then go to his office until class was over. For evaluation night, however, he came with us to the office of Ms. Success.

Whatever she was doing, it seemed to be working. While Dad's office was in one of the old, drafty buildings with crooked doors, Ms. Success was in the newly built ivory tower, where all the inner doors were cherry wood with chrome handles. The placard on her door actually read "Ms. Success," and I could hear Nick snicker into his hand.

Dad nudged my brother and knocked.

"Come," said a woman's voice. It was loud, authoritative, and almost masculine.

Dad poked his head into the room, and the woman's

voice sounded even louder. "Jaaake!" She stretched out Dad's first name. "How the heck are ya?"

"Just fine, Sharon. I've brought my kids." Dad held the door open wider and motioned for us to step inside.

Ms. Success was tall with a hawklike nose and enormous brown eyes that made her look slightly cartoonish. Her brown hair was cropped short against her head, and she was sitting behind a massive glass desk.

Ms. Success smiled at us, revealing a predatory amount of teeth, and got to her feet.

"Well, well. This must be Nick, Parker, and Alexis." She pointed to all of us in turn.

"Alex," I corrected.

"It's Alexis," said Emily, coming in behind us. "We already made your T-shirt." She held up a blue shirt as proof, showing me the back. My name had been printed above the number one, like a sports jersey.

"Yep. Alexis," I said, taking the shirt from her with a tight smile. "And it's blue."

Blue was Mom's favorite color. Her entire office—curtains, carpet, paintings—had something blue in each part of it. *I* loved black, even though Parker had pointed out on several occasions that it was actually the absence of all color.

"It's nice though, right, Alex?" Nick elbowed me and nodded encouragingly.

33

I turned the shirt over. On the front was the same smiling star from the pamphlet, but this time in an Olympic-style jumpsuit. Above the star were the words CHUMPS ARE LAME . . . , and below the star, CHAMPS GOT GAME!

"Wow," I said. "It's . . . really something."

Emily handed Nick and Parker theirs, introducing herself as she went. "I'm Emily Gold. I'm one of Alexis's friends from school, and I'm the Champs coaching assistant."

"And I, of course, am your coach." Ms. Success winked at us. "But I'm sure you already guessed that."

"Ms. Success," I said. "Is . . . is that your real last name?"

"Alex . . . ," said Dad.

Ms. Success held up her hand and smiled. "It's fine. I get that question *all* the time because of who I am and how well I do."

I exchanged a doubtful glance with my brothers while Ms. Success strolled around her desk. "Success really *is* my last name. Sharon Success." She gave a small laugh that barely lifted her shoulders. "You might even say I'm *sharin' success* with you." She fired finger guns at my brothers and me, one after the other, and Nick could barely contain his laughter.

Thankfully, Ms. Success assumed he was amused by her joke, so she smirked and went back to her seat.

34

"Jake, why don't you and the kids relax while I take a peek at those surveys." She pointed to a row of folding chairs against the wall that looked out of place in the plush office. Dad handed her the papers, and we all sat and waited nervously.

Just like Dad, Ms. Success frowned as she read through the papers, shuffling them and re-reading them several times. Occasionally, she turned the pages sideways and upside down, maybe hoping to shake out *good* answers.

To keep from going crazy, I stopped watching her and grabbed a framed group photo off a bookshelf beside me.

"That's the current class," said Emily, crouching next to me. She pointed to a guy in the back row of the picture and lowered her voice. "And that's Trevor," she whispered with a little grin. "He's—"

Before she could explain, Ms. Success cleared her throat and put the surveys down, folding her hands in front of her. Emily stood and so did the rest of us, as if Ms. Success were some judge giving a ruling.

"It's nice to meet you kids," said Ms. Success, smiling with all her teeth again. "I like your father, and I want to like you. However . . ." She made a clicking sound in the corner of her mouth. "We've got a lot of work to do."

"We had a feeling that might be the case," said Dad.

Ms. Success looked at the paper on top. "Nick."

My brother sat up straight. "Yes, ma'am."

"You're athletic and you've got great social skills, but . . . it might not hurt you to get a tutor. Or at least someone who can tell you the difference between depression and the Great Depression." She pulled out a thick black marker and circled the intellectual portion, sliding the paper to the edge of her desk.

Nick blushed and retrieved it. "Yes, ma'am."

"Parker!" She practically barked his name, and he jumped. "No running, swimming, or otherwise useful skills, but you've got the sarcasm down. You strike me as a very bright, funny guy."

He relaxed and smiled.

Ms. Success shook her head. "Too bad bright and funny won't keep the enemies from tying bricks to your ankles and throwing you in the lake."

Parker stared at her, wide-eyed. "Huh?"

"Um, Sharon?" said Dad.

She held her hands up. "I apologize. That was a bit extreme. Worst case scenario." She circled the physical portion of his paper and slid it over. "Your hair would probably help with buoyancy. I'm sure you'd be okay."

"Yes, Ms. . . . Coach . . . Success," he stammered.

"And finally we get to Miss Alexis," she said, fanning herself with my paper. "You're smart and active enough, and you're friends with Emily, which is a plus." She nodded to her stepdaughter, who grinned and stood with her hands on her hips like a superhero. "But I question your involvement in *The Breakfast Club* since a, it was fictional, and b, it was well before your time. Let's make some real friends, okay?"

Once I'd gotten my paper back, Ms. Success nodded to Emily, who came forward with three identical books entitled *The Secrets of Success*. The cover featured none other than Ms. Success, hands held out with palms up, balancing the words "you" and "winner."

"I'm sure you learned a little about the Champs philosophy from our pamphlet," said Ms. Success. She took the books from Emily and opened each one to the front page. With a ballpoint pen, she autographed them for us while she kept talking.

"Any child can be a champ if they have a balanced life and the skills to help them excel. I'm here to teach you those skills." She handed over the books. "This is your life material. It'll come in handy well beyond your days in my class. Maybe even as a flotation device." She pointed to Parker and winked.

He glowered at her, but she didn't notice, already having moved on to the binders Emily was now passing out.

"Your class schedules are in there, as well as worksheets and progress forms," said Ms. Success. "Every session, we'll touch on a different skill. Last week's were Time Management and Adventures in Organization, which I'll review in a bit. Are there any questions so far?"

Parker raised his hand. "How are we graded?"

"The same as in life," said Ms. Success. She squinted in a way that was probably meant to seem contemplative, but actually looked more like constipated. "You're graded by whether or not you succeed."

I wrinkled my forehead. "So . . . this is a pass/fail course?"

Emily sucked in her breath and Ms. Success winced. "We don't like to use the *f* word around here, Alexis. Fail, can't, impossible: Those are chump words that don't belong in a champ's vocabulary."

It took an unnatural amount of willpower not to roll my eyes. "Sorry." I pointed to Dad. "But he says we *all* have to pass the class. We just want to know what it's going to take."

Ms. Success frowned and lowered her voice. "Are you talking about a bribe, Ms. Evins? You think slipping me a few Benjamins will get you a passing grade?"

"Uh, no," I said.

"Oh." Ms. Success sounded slightly disappointed. "Then your best bet is to show up for every class, work hard, and make it to the Champs Championship, since that's fifty percent of your grade."

"Championship?" repeated Parker, always up for a little competition. "What's that?"

"It's a culmination of everything you'll learn in this class," said Ms. Success. "You start with fund-raising the three hundred dollar team entry fee and then move on to the competition."

"What if we *can't* raise the money?" asked Nick. "Do we *fail*?"

Ms. Success brought a hand to her chest and grimaced, as if my brother were killing her with his chump words. "In my class, you'll learn the skills necessary to make that money. I guarantee it."

"So, what's the competition?" asked Parker. "A quiz bowl? Brainteasers? Puzzles?"

Ms. Success studied him for a moment, then leaned back in her cushiony leather chair. "Life is a rat race, and you're caught in the maze, Mr. Evins. You have to be smart enough to find the cheese, quick enough to outrun the other rats, and friendly enough that they don't try to bite off your tail when it's over."

Everyone in my family looked at one another, mystified.

"So, the championship is a giant maze?" asked Nick.

"It's a combination of things," said Ms. Success, bringing her hands together. "Trust, mixed with leadership, sprinkled with—"

"It's an obstacle course," said Emily. "And a fire-building contest."

Ms. Success pointed at Emily. "That too."

"It sounds kind of cool," said Nick, smiling.

"It is cooler than an Eskimo's freezer," said Ms. Success. "And the winning team receives a thousand dollars."

Money signs flashed in the greedy eyes of all of us Evil Evins.

"I think," Dad said, "you now have their undivided attention."

"Glad to hear it," said Ms. Success. "Why don't we review Adventures in Organization?"

My brothers and I all flipped open our books and binders.

"I'd like to start by sharing a personal philosophy with you," she said, resting her chin on her fingertips. "Get organized . . . or get lost."

Two hours later, my brothers and I stumbled out of Ms. Success's office looking like victims of a zombie attack. Dad, on the other hand, almost cartwheeled into the hallway.

"This is going to be excellent!" He herded us toward the exit. "I'll admit, I initially had misgivings—"

"Please . . ." Nick clutched Dad's arm. "I can't take any more big words."

"Or positive energy," I said. "I just want to put on black lipstick and hang out with emo kids."

Dad threw an arm around our shoulders. "I know it's a lot to process, but that's only because you're behind in class."

"Uh, no." Nick scoffed. "I've been behind in classes before. This is just the first time I've ever wanted to climb into a wood chipper."

Dad raised an eyebrow. "I think that's a bit extreme."

"These homework activities are extreme," said Parker. "Have you seen the time schedule she expects us to follow? I'll only have ten minutes for my hair!"

"And she wants us to raise three hundred dollars!" said Nick. "Except for my allowance, the only money I've ever earned, I've found in the couch."

Dad turned hopefully to me. "Alex, what do you think?"

I glanced down at my Champs gear, then up at Dad. "Do you want me to be honest, or do you want me to be nice?"

"You can't do both?"

"Not without electroshock therapy," I said.

Dad's eyebrows knitted, but he forced a smile. "Come on. This is going to be excellent. Remember what Ralph Waldo Emerson said, 'Nothing great was ever achieved without *enthusiasm*'!" He punched each of my brothers playfully in the shoulder.

41

Parker, of course, fell down.

"I guess we really *should* work on your physical conditioning," said Dad, helping him to his feet.

"That's my problem with this whole thing," said Nick. "Ms. Success wants us to improve ourselves, but . . . How am I supposed to suddenly get smarter?"

"You could try doing your homework," said Dad.

"And listening in class," said Parker.

"And taking notes," I said.

Nick looked thoughtful. "Or maybe there's a pill. . . ."

"You're getting a tutor," said Dad, opening the door that led outside. "And you . . ."—he pointed at me—"are joining some clubs to work on your social skills."

I stopped in my tracks. "But I'm already going to a slumber party! With awkward conversations about boys and feelings. Isn't that enough?"

"That's one night," said Dad. "Even less if you pretend to be deaf or asleep, which I wouldn't put past you."

"Fine." I got into the backseat of the car. "I'll look at the list of clubs tomorrow."

"I want you to sign up for two," said Dad.

"Sure," I said. I'd join as many as he wanted. It didn't mean I was going to participate.

"And I want signed proof that you were at the meetings," he added.

I slammed my door, wishing Dad wasn't so smart sometimes.

"What about Parker?" I pointed out, blocking a slap my brother aimed at my head. "He's a weakling."

"Don't worry about your brother," said Dad. "I'll come up with something."

"Just so you know, I refuse to sweat," Parker spoke up. "It makes my hair look strange."

"I don't think it's sweat doing that," I said.

This time Parker succeeded in punching my shoulder. "See? I'm not a weakling."

Nick glanced back from the front passenger seat. "Yeah, good job. You can beat up a twelve-year-old girl."

Parker yawned and leaned back. "It still counts as physical activity."

"You can't count hitting your sister as physical activity, Parker." Dad pulled out of the campus lot. "Not unless you chase her for a while first."

"Dad!" I laughed and pushed the back of his seat.

He winked at me in the rearview mirror. "I promise, this is going to be—"

"Excellent," my brothers and I chorused.

"See?" said Dad with a grin. "You're already thinking like a team."

✾ Chapter 4

Apparently, Dad's idea of excellence was waking his children up for school with the terrifying blast of an air horn.

HOOOOOOOOOONK!

"Get up, get up! We're on a tight schedule!" Dad called into my room before sprinting down the hall.

HOOOOOOOOONK!

I opened my eyes and saw nothing but white.

"Wha—?" I gasped in confusion and almost sucked a sheet of paper into my throat.

Dad had taped a note to my forehead.

I ripped it off and flipped it over, squinting blearily at what was written on the other side.

7:00 Get up!

7:02 Evacuate.

7:05 Shower.

I groaned when I realized this was the exact schedule laid out in Ms. Success's book. Dad had picked Tuesday morning to practice the time management exercise.

"Alex!" Dad popped his head into my doorway again. "Get up! You're already behind!"

Nick appeared beside him, looking as irritated as I felt. "Why do we have to evacuate?" he asked. "Did Alex set *our* house on fire this time?"

I chucked my pillow at him, then got up to retrieve it when I realized I'd need it for sleep.

Dad saw me making the crawl back to the covers and grabbed my arm. "No you don't. Time to get up. And Nick, 'evacuate' is a nicer way of saying 'use the restroom.'"

Nick squinted for a moment, and then his eyes widened. "Ohhh. Like evacuating your body of . . . I only get three minutes for that?!"

"Well, yes. It's not supposed to be a leisure activity," said Dad.

"I think I have someone else's schedule," said Parker, rubbing his eyes as he stumbled toward us. "Mine says, 'Seven twenty . . . Apply makeup.'"

Nick and I looked at our schedules.

"Mine says 'Groom facial hair,'" said Nick.

I frowned. "So does mine."

Parker leaned close to study me. "I was wondering when someone was going to mention your mustache."

"Shut up!" I covered my upper lip and pushed him with my free hand.

Dad took both our schedules, glanced at them, and swapped them. "Sorry about that. Now, everyone get moving. It's"—he glanced at his watch—"seven ten and none of you have even gone to the bathroom yet!"

"Evacuated," Nick corrected Dad.

Dad fixed him with a stare.

"And I'm gone," said Nick, hurrying away.

"Alex, use my bathroom," said Dad. "Parker, the guest bathroom." Dad headed for the stairs. "Everyone needs to be dressed and at the breakfast table in twenty minutes."

"For a guy who sometimes stirs his coffee with a pen, Dad's irritatingly together this morning," grumbled Parker.

I smiled but didn't answer. Now that I was waking up, I kind of liked the extra attention from Dad. And the fact that his suspenders were actually holding up pants this time, and not pajamas, was a good sign.

Since I never took long in the shower and I didn't wear makeup, I whipped in and out of the bathroom, threw on some jeans and a T-shirt, and headed downstairs.

Dad applauded when he saw me. "First one for breakfast, with five minutes to spare!"

I bowed at the waist. "Nick's right behind me, but I think Parker's still in the shower. He probably won't be down until after you leave for work."

Most mornings Dad waited until he saw us downstairs at breakfast before he left the house. The occasional exceptions were for Parker's epic hair battles or when Nick forgot his homework and bribed Parker to do it. Yesterday had been different because of our Champs surveys, but I expected Dad wouldn't make that a habit.

"I'm sure your brother will be down *very* soon," said Dad, flipping through the paper. "Mainly because I turned off the water heater."

A moment later, we could hear Parker shrieking. I smirked at Dad, who hid a smile behind a sip of coffee.

Nick strolled into the kitchen, wincing. "Parker can really hit those high notes. You turned off the hot water?"

"I did," said Dad.

Nick shook his head. "You know that's not going to speed up his styling process. He'll probably move even slower just to make you mad."

Dad looked unconcerned. "Parker loves school too much to miss it."

And he was right. Fifteen minutes later, when Nick and I were finishing breakfast, Parker stomped downstairs, fluffy hair and all.

"That . . . was cruel," he growled at Dad, before continuing his march of gloom to the refrigerator.

"But you had plenty of time to do your hair," I pointed out.

Parker wheeled around to glare at me. "*What* are you talking about? My hair is a nightmare!"

I wrinkled my forehead. "It looks the same as always."

"Uh, nooo. It's an inch shorter because I didn't have time to volumize!"

Everyone at the table watched him quietly. After a pause, Nick and I glanced at each other.

Then we burst out laughing.

"It's not funny!" roared Parker.

"Dude, please," Nick sputtered. "Tell me you *don't* measure your hair every day."

"It's no weirder than you hitting on girls," said Parker, his face reddening. "Or Alex keeping pennies that she finds on the ground. Even the ones in public restrooms!"

"Yeah." Nick turned on me. "That's gross!"

"They're good luck!" I argued.

"Not if you get E. coli and die."

"All right, that's enough," said Dad. "You're each very special and I don't want you to stop being who you are." He cleared his throat. "Although, Alex, you should probably let the housekeeper sanitize those pennies."

"Fine," I said, carrying my dishes to the sink.

Emily's head popped up in the window just as I reached it.

"Augh!" I screamed, almost dropping my plate.

"Everything okay?" called Dad.

"Yeah." I pressed my hand to my heart. "Nothing serious." I glared at Emily and opened the kitchen window. "I have easy access to several sharp knives. Speak."

"I need your help," she said. "Can you meet me outside when you're ready? Please?"

I knew Emily's stubborn nature meant she wouldn't leave until she'd had her say. At least this time I wasn't in a bathroom stall.

"Fine," I said with a sigh.

"And you might want to trim back these bushes," she said. "I almost couldn't make it to the window."

I fixed her with a stare.

"I'll just be on the porch," she said quickly, and hurried away.

Back at the table, Dad was packing up for work.

"Who was that?" he asked.

"Emily," I said. "She wanted to talk before school."

"Sure she did," said Parker with a snort. "I'll bet Ms. Success sent her to spy on us."

Nick checked out the window. "I wondered what that surveillance van was doing across the street."

I rolled my eyes. "Whatever."

"It'd be less obvious without the Champs star on the side."

"Shut up!" I said, laughing now.

"All right, everyone, I've got a meeting in . . ." Dad checked his watch and winced. "Half an hour ago. So be good at school." He pointed at Parker. "Pay attention in class." He pointed at Nick. "And get some extracurriculars." He kissed me on the forehead. "I'll see all of you tonight."

And with that he was gone.

The second the door clicked behind Dad, Parker jumped out of his chair. "I need to brush my teeth!" he blurted, and dashed upstairs.

Nick looked at me. "Do you think he's volumizing?"

I nodded. "Yep."

"Do you think I should stop him?"

"If you're tired of living, sure." I got up from the table. "I have to meet Emily. Good luck."

"Yeah, you too," said Nick, grabbing a pot lid and holding it in front of him like a shield. Before the Battle of the Evins could begin, I grabbed my backpack and stepped out to join Emily.

"All right, what's the drama?" I asked.

Instantly, she turned pink. "There's this boy."

I cringed. Emily was going to talk about her love life. I was neither prepared *nor* interested in having this conversation.

"Look, I don't have a boyfriend," I told her. "I'm not the best person to offer romantic advice."

"I don't have a boyfriend either," she said. "Not yet. That's why I need your help."

"Why?" I leaned in. "Are you in love with one of my brothers?"

Emily's face twisted into a grimace. "Ew! No."

"Ahem." I pulled back and crossed my arms. "That's my family you're talking about. You could do a *lot* worse."

"Sorry," she said.

"I mean, we've got naturally great teeth." I flashed my whites at her. "And we don't look it, but we've got excellent knees."

"*Fine*," she said, stepping off the porch. "Can we get back to me?"

"Right." I followed her out to the sidewalk. "So you like some guy."

"Trevor," she whispered. "The one from the picture in my stepmom's office. He's in your Champs class."

I lowered my voice too. "Why are you being so secretive?"

51

"Other girls from school take this path," said Emily. "And if they heard me talk about how amazing Trevor is, they'd hunt him down and—"

"Kill him?" I asked, widening my eyes in mock fear.

Emily gave me a withering look. "Try to steal him away. But I have a genuine interest in Trevor. I'm the best girl for him."

"Well, good." I clapped her on the back. "The world needs more decent, *modest* people like you."

She ignored my sarcasm. "The thing is, I don't want him to meet you and fall in love with you."

I stopped and stared at Emily. "Wow. Where did *that* come from?"

To answer, she reached into her backpack and pulled out a spiral notebook. The front cover was smattered with glitter hearts surrounding the letters PT.

"Um, what is that?" I asked.

"Project Trevor," she said in a no-nonsense voice. "It's everything I know about him. And so far you two seem highly compatible."

I took the notebook from her and flipped through several ink-filled pages, some of which included magazine clippings about stuff I assumed Trevor was into.

I gave her a concerned look. "You don't, uh, have a shrine to him too, do you?"

Emily snatched back her notebook. "Don't be stupid. I just think it's important to know everything you can about someone before you attempt to establish a relationship."

I started to nod, then paused. "Wait . . . do you have one of those notebooks on me?"

"No," Emily sniffed. "Everything of interest about you fits on an index card."

"Nice," I said wryly. "And you don't have to worry about me stealing him away. Since you like him, I'll consider him off-limits."

Emily nodded and started walking again, but she didn't look particularly relieved.

Against my better judgment, I asked, "Is there something else?"

Emily kicked a rock out of her path and let out a huge sigh. "Even if you leave him alone, it won't matter. I don't think he notices me as more than a teacher's aide."

"Maybe you're not doing anything to draw his attention," I said, nodding toward the notebook. "You have plenty of information on Trevor, some of which I'm sure the government doesn't even know. Pick something you have in common and talk about it."

"That's just it!" Emily waved her notebook in exasperation. "We have *nothing* in common, other than how extremely clever and cute we both are." She flipped to a dog-eared page and jabbed at it. "He likes Cheetos dipped in chocolate pudding. I tried that and I almost threw up!"

"Probably because it's gross," I said.

"He also likes to watch science-fiction movies, so I tried *Star Wars*," said Emily. "Explain to me how a rebel space pilot and his ten-foot dog can afford fuel for their starship when they're always running from creditors!"

I smiled. "I think you're missing the point of the movie."

Emily smacked herself in the forehead with her notebook. "My stepmom's right. The best guys are the ones in comas."

I took the notebook back from her. "Look. Start with something simple." I scanned a page. "He likes the Ankle Biters. You have to like them. They're a great band."

"Their lead singer sounds like he's being tortured with a weed whacker," she said. "Plus, you can't understand the lyrics. Even if you play the CD backward."

"That's the beauty!" I said. "You can interpret their music any way you want."

"I already do," said Emily. "As garbage."

I sighed. "You have to give a little somewhere. If you don't like the same things as Trevor, at least ask him *why* he likes them. It'll help you understand him better."

Emily gripped my arms and smiled. "That's clever. I can dissect his personality and see the different layers."

"Exactly! Just don't tell him you plan to dissect him," I said, handing back the notebook. "That tends to freak people out."

She laughed. "Thanks, Alexis. And if you wouldn't mind . . ." Emily bowed her head.

"This conversation never happened," I said. "Not that anybody would ever believe that I'd given love advice."

"Good." *Now* the usual bounce returned to both Emily's step and ponytail. "Hey, so you looked kind of sick when you left my stepmom's office yesterday. Are you okay?"

I shrugged. "Aside from the night terrors and vomiting? Yes."

"Alexis!"

"I'm kidding. But are the classes always so intense?"

Emily squinted thoughtfully. "If by intense, you mean fabulous and awesome—"

"I don't."

She acted as if she didn't hear me. "Then yes. Tonight's will be just as intense. My stepmom is *very* passionate about what she does."

I nodded. "Like a cult leader."

Emily frowned. "That's not funny."

"Sorry," I said.

We reached the school and I hesitated at the entrance. To sign up for clubs, I'd have to visit the counselor's office. Ms.

Dorf had been waiting there to talk family issues since I'd started junior high.

"Hey!" I said brightly to Emily. "You know what would be fun? Going to the counselor's office together."

Ms. Dorf couldn't *possibly* expect me to discuss personal issues in front of someone else. I linked my arm through Emily's the way I'd seen girls do with friends.

"Um, okay," she said. "But why?"

"I'm joining some clubs. You know, to work on my 'social skills.'" I put the words in air quotes.

Oddly enough, *that* seemed genuinely exciting to her. Emily beamed and jerked me into a fast walk. "Which clubs?"

I shrugged. "Whichever ones meet today."

She slowed a little to look at me. "You're joking."

"If I had a choice, I wouldn't be doing this at all," I said. "But apparently going to Chloe's party isn't enough of a social effort. Not even if I braid everyone's hair."

"You're going to the slumber party?" Emily clutched my arm, a smile tugging at the corners of her mouth.

I was kind of afraid to say yes in case she dismembered me in her excitement, but when I didn't respond, she almost pulled my arm out of its socket anyway.

"Are you?" she asked.

"Ow! Yes!"

Emily squealed and threw her arms around me. "We're going to have so much fun at Chloe's!"

I patted her shoulder. "If she has firecrackers and an old toilet, we'll certainly try."

Emily freed herself and knocked on the door to the counselor's office.

Ms. Dorf poked her head out. "Hello, Emily!" She turned to me with confusion. "And Alexis. What a nice surprise! Are you here to . . ." She paused. "What can I do for you?"

"I'm not here to talk about my mom, first of all," I said. "She's not a part of my life anymore."

Ms. Dorf smiled gently. "Oh, I think your mom's a bigger part of your life than you realize."

I shook my head. "Whatever. I'm here for extracurriculars. Can you help me?"

"Of course." Ms. Dorf pulled the door open.

While Emily and I sat, Ms. Dorf grabbed a list of school clubs off her desk. "I have to say, I'm pleased to finally see you taking an interest in social activities, Alexis. What are you considering?"

"How about . . ." I closed my eyes and stabbed randomly at the paper. When I pulled back my finger to reveal my selection, I said, "French club."

Ms. Dorf looked slightly less pleased. "I really hope you don't make all of your decisions that way."

"No, usually there's a dartboard involved," I said.

Emily kicked me and forced herself to laugh. "She's just fooling around, Ms. Dorf. Alexis was telling me she's actually interested in . . ." Emily's eyes skipped down the page, then back up to Ms. Dorf. "In robotics club."

"Right," I said. "And the . . . hockey boosters."

Emily curled her lip. "Really?"

I shrugged. "Violence on ice. What's not to love?"

Ms. Dorf leaned toward me. "Alexis, I know I haven't seen you much, but I don't think those clubs are right for you. Are you sure there's nothing else you'd rather try?"

When she saw me close my eyes and point my finger again, she stopped me. "All right. Robotics club meets after school, but hockey boosters meet during study hall, so I'll have to give you a pass for that."

"Great!" I said. "I bet I'll love it."

Chapter 5 ✿

I t was a good thing I didn't actually put money on that bet. When I got to the hockey boosters meeting, the room was filled with giggling girls, loud pop music, and the stench of wet paint.

There was no ice, no violence. There weren't even any missing teeth strewn about.

"Um, hello?" I called.

The girls glanced up, but only one of them actually came over.

Chloe Stroupe.

"Hey, Alex! Are you looking for someone?" she asked.

"Actually, I'm here to join the boosters," I said, thrusting a piece of paper at her. "Will you sign this as proof I came?"

Chloe didn't move. "*You're* joining the boosters?"

"Sure." I shrugged. "I like hockey and I figured it'd be nice to meet some other, uh, fans." I wondered if that was even the right word. Several of the girls were now singing into the hockey sticks like microphones, my slumber party nightmare come true.

Chloe crossed her arms and smirked. "And this wouldn't have anything to do with Champs?"

I sighed and pulled back my paper. "Emily got to you first, huh?"

Chloe laughed. "She didn't tell me. I get the Champs newsletter."

My eyebrows rose a little. The newsletter wasn't a surprise. I wouldn't have put it past Ms. Success to write her announcements in nightly fireworks. But the fact that anyone at school besides Emily would ever go to that class. . . .

"You're in Champs too?" I asked.

Chloe nodded. "You know me. I'm in it to win it. Plus, my parents want me to get into a good college some day. Hey!" She bumped my arm. "Do you have a team for the Champs Championship?"

"Oh! Um, I hadn't even thought about it," I said. "But I doubt my brothers want me on theirs. So . . . no."

"You'll be on *my* team then," she said confidently. "You're a pretty good athlete . . . when you're not playing badminton. And I *really* want that thousand dollars."

"Okay," I said with a shrug. "Sounds like a plan."

"Great! It'll be you, me, and . . . hopefully *Trevor.*" She sighed and took on a wistful expression.

"Trevor?" My ears pricked up, but I tried to act nonchalant. "Who's Trevor?"

"Just this really cute guy in our class." She pressed her hands to her heart and smiled blissfully. "I am sooo crushing on him."

This had disaster written all over it.

"You know you shouldn't let feelings cloud your judgment," I said.

Chloe's dreamy expression vanished. "Nice message. Is that from an *anti*-Valentine card?"

"Actually, my mom . . ." I paused, remembering what Ms. Dorf had said earlier. I shook her words out of my head. "Emotions are a distraction from reaching your goals."

"But Trevor's such a cute distraction," said Chloe with a sigh. Any second, little cartoon hearts would start bubbling up around her.

"That nice, huh?" I wondered how many other girls were in love with Trevor. "Guess I'll have to check him out."

Instantly the little cartoon hearts around Chloe frosted over, along with her eyes. "I'd rather you didn't," she said in a steely voice. "I know you're not super familiar with the girl

61

universe, but stealing another girl's crush is the worst thing you could *ever* do."

"Whoa, wait!" I held up my hands in submission. "I didn't mean anything like that."

"Oh." Chloe must have realized how chainsaw-wielding psycho she sounded because she laughed with an apologetic shrug. "Sorry! I know you're not one of *those* girls. And, I mean, it's not like you could take him from me anyway."

"Right," I said, racking my brain for a change of subject. "So, Ms. Success told you about me and my brothers?"

Chloe relaxed a little more. "Yes, in *The Shout Out*. She sends it every Wednesday and Friday, although for you and your brothers, there was a special issue last night."

"Wow. My dad always figured we'd be in the news someday," I said. "He'll be glad to know the words 'crime spree' weren't involved."

Chloe grinned and tugged my arm. "Come on. You can help with one of the banners for Saturday's game."

"I'm not really artistic," I said.

"That's okay. The banners are just an excuse to go crazy with glitter glue and get out of homeroom." She reached into a cardboard supply box and pulled out two shimmering tubes. "Pick your poison."

But I wondered if teaming up with her for Champs meant I already had.

"You look like you went through my kind of day," Nick said when I entered the living room that afternoon. His eyes were red, and he rubbed them tiredly.

"Actually, you look worse." I sprawled on the floor next to his couch. "What happened?"

Nick sipped from a mug between his hands and winced. "I couldn't sleep last night and then I forced myself to stay awake all day in class so I could listen and take notes."

"Awww, Nick!" I punched him playfully in the leg. "I'm so proud."

My brother smirked and took another drink. "I didn't say I succeeded."

"Oh." I frowned. "What went wrong?"

"Well, it turns out my first period teacher has some sort of funny accent—"

"Where from?"

"Texas, I think. And then in second period, I couldn't see the notes on the board, so I started copying off the girl next to me. She thought I was watching her, we got to talking, and . . ." He sighed. "Now I have a date for Friday's game but no clue how mitosis works." He lifted the mug to his lips, jammed his eyes shut, and drank again.

"What *is* that?" I reached up and tilted the cup toward me. When I peered inside I saw a pool of brown sludge.

"I made coffee," said Nick.

"Are you sure?" I asked, watching the goop slosh from side to side. "It looks like you just . . . poured hot water over coffee grounds."

"I did," he said. "I made coffee before I realized I didn't know how." He looked from his mug to me. "We're going to be shipped off to St. Ignatius. I'm too stupid for Champs."

I thumped him hard on the arm. "No, you're not! Don't say that. Besides, if anyone's going to make us fail, it's me and my unsocial skills."

Nick sucked in his breath. "Right. You had to do the club thing. How'd that go?"

"I went to the hockey boosters meeting and robotics club," I said.

"Robotics?" asked Nick. "That's kind of cool."

"You'd think so," I said. "But no. It turns out *this* robotics club doesn't build robots—they talk like them."

Nick snorted. "What?!"

"Yeah." I pressed my lips together. "A group of really, *really* nerdy guys sit in a circle and speak 'Robot' to one another."

"As in 'beep-beep-boop'?" asked Nick, grinning.

"Nope. They babble a long string of ones and zeros. It's called binary, but *I* call it a slow, painful death."

Nick laughed. "Okay then, how was hockey boosters?"

"Well, the girls think a Zamboni is a sports car, and they

64

haven't ever been to an *entire* game because their hot cocoa runs out after the first period."

Nick made a face. "Sorry."

"If Dad actually expects me to stick to these clubs, I'm in trouble," I said.

"Maybe you could drop out after Champs is over," he said.

"If I wait *that* long, it might be hazardous to the boosters' health," I said. "But at least they're good at coming up with fund-raising ideas. I might borrow one or two for my Champs Championship entry fee."

"That's a good idea," said Nick. "I talked to my coach since he's big on supporting his students, and he said he'd think about ways I can help him out to raise my money, too."

I smiled. "Maybe we could just sell Parker's hair and split the profit."

"Who would buy it?" Nick snorted. "Halloween's still months away."

We both laughed, and I looked around. "Speaking of Parker, where is he?" I asked.

"He's convinced that whatever physical activity Dad has planned will turn him into a hideous man-beast, so he's spending as much time with Ashley as possible."

I lay back down. "At least he got *some* enjoyment out of the day."

No sooner had I said the words than we heard the front door slam. Several times.

"Uh-oh," said Nick.

"Hey, if a group of angry Parkers just came in, can one of them get me a soda?" I called.

"And teach me how to make coffee?" asked Nick.

Parker appeared in the doorway, red-faced and scowling. "Ashley and I broke up today. Ask me for a favor again. I dare you." Then he threw down his backpack and stormed into the kitchen.

Nick and I got up and followed him.

"How did it happen?" asked Nick.

"I told her about Champs and how hard it was to keep up with the schedule *and* still have time for my hair. Then she said I spent too much time on my appearance."

"What'd *you* say?" I prompted.

Parker's angry expression slipped away a little, and he blushed. "That maybe she didn't spend *enough* time on hers."

Nick and I both winced.

"Ouch," said Nick. "So she broke up with you because you insulted her?"

"Well, that and because I got upset about her comment." He reached into the refrigerator and grabbed a soda. "She said I wasn't seeing the big picture."

"How could you with all that hair?" I asked.

Parker downed half the soda in one swallow. "I'm gonna need a couple of these bad boys to dull the pain."

Nick yawned and slapped Parker on the shoulder. "Drink them while you get ready. Dad'll be home soon to take us to Champs."

"I'm ready now," said Parker.

"No, Dad wants us to change into our special T-shirts," said Nick. "He says all the students are wearing theirs for our welcome."

"Fantastic," said Parker, slamming the soda can on the counter. "I'm single and my Champs wardrobe guarantees I'll stay that way."

The three of us tossed our dignity aside and changed into the blue cotton T-shirts with freakish stars on them. When Dad came home, he took one look at us and said, "I know things seem tough, but as the old saying goes, 'It's always darkest before the dawn.'"

Nick groaned and buried his head in his hands. "It's going to get even worse *tonight*?"

Dad cleared his throat. "I actually meant things will get better."

"Easy for you to say!" I exclaimed. "You're not trying to convince a group of girls that hockey sticks don't work like microphones!"

"And you don't know how hard it is to stay awake when

they're serving turkey sandwiches and warm milk for lunch in the cafeteria!" said Nick.

"And my girlfriend broke up with me!" blurted Parker.

Dad just stood there, looking sheepish. "See? What could be even worse than all of those things?"

"Going to Champs," I said.

But Dad still made us get in the car.

At least he knew better than to say "have fun" when he dropped us off in front of the building. My brothers and I looked at one another, gave a collective sigh, and forged ahead into the ivory tower.

Ms. Success was standing just inside the door, talking into a headset. When she saw us, she smiled and indicated that we should follow her.

"Well, that's fantastic, Jimbo!" she boomed into the mouthpiece. "Tell DreamWorks we can do lunch, but only at the Four Seasons. I'm not suffering through another rank cheese platter like I did with Nickelodeon."

I wondered at first if there was even anyone on the other end of the line, but then I distinctly heard a male voice squawking from the headset.

"Is she really talking to a studio exec?" asked Nick.

"It's probably her confused gardener," I whispered back. "All he did was call to ask about the roses, and now he's trapped in her world of make-believe."

Nick and Parker both snickered, but the three of us sobered quickly when Ms. Success stopped and turned to face us. We were standing outside a door with "Champs!" written across it, not with construction paper, but with *brass* lettering.

Ms. Success laughed into the mouthpiece and winked at us. "All right then, Jimmer-Jam. I'll talk to you later. I've got some minds to blow." She pulled off the headset and gave us all a quick once-over.

"Evins kids! You look fantastic. Blue's a power color on you."

"Uh, we *feel* powerful," said Nick with a big smile.

She pointed at him. "I'll bet you do, even with all that dirt in your teeth."

"Dirt?" Nick ran his tongue around his mouth and groaned, ducking away to the water fountain.

Ms. Success sidled closer to me. "Your brother doesn't eat cement too, does he?" she asked in a low voice. "Because I know a guy with the circus—"

"Nick wasn't eating dirt," I said, resisting the urge to roll my eyes. "He was drinking coffee grounds."

"No filters at home, huh?" She nodded down the hall. "Go ahead and nab a few from the break room. I won't say a word."

"Oh, no thanks," I said.

69

"Alexis." Ms. Success put a hand on my shoulder. "If you want to survive in the business world, you've got to accept perks as they come to you. Knowing me," she said with a wink, "is a perk."

I bit my tongue and summoned a smile. "Gosh, I don't know what to say. I mean, free coffee filters. . . ."

Ms. Success waved away the thanks I hadn't planned to give. "Grab yourself a couple bags of microwave popcorn while you're at it."

"We're okay," I said. "Really."

She patted me on the head. "All right, kiddo. Then are you ready to mix it up with your fellow Champs?" She shimmied from side to side.

"Not if we have to dance like that," said Parker.

Ms. Success turned toward him wearing a frown, and I stepped in front of my brother.

"Sorry. His girlfriend just broke up with him."

"Oh, ouch!" Ms. Success squeezed his shoulder and clucked her tongue sympathetically. "That's tough, but there are plenty of other fish in the sea. Who knows? You might even land a ten-pounder in *there*!" She grinned and gestured toward the classroom.

"I don't even know what that means," said Parker. "What girl weighs ten pounds?"

Ms. Success blinked at him then clapped her hands.

"Okaaay! Let's get this party started. Wait right here for me to announce you."

"Can't we just . . . walk into the classroom?" I asked.

Ms. Success gave an amused scoff. "No, Alexis! You're a Champ now. And Champs deserve to be noticed. Now, let's all put on our best faces and wow the crowd, okay?"

Ms. Success threw open the door, and the entire class broke into applause.

"Ladies and gentlemen," she announced, "welcome our newest Champs, the Energetic Evins!"

❀ Chapter 6

I frowned at my brothers. "Did she just call us energetic?"

I was never energetic. Not even after five Red Bulls and a bowl of sugar. Parker maybe had a "whoo!" in him, and Nick was probably good for a chest bump, but we'd certainly never been considered lively.

Ms. Success turned to us from the doorway with a huge grin and gave an over-the-top hand wave to gesture us inside.

I pulled my brothers close for a quick conference. "So, are we going for energetic?"

"I think we have to," Nick said. "Otherwise, we'll look like idiots after all that applause." He turned away from me. "Jump onto my back and start whooping."

"Yeah, because *that* doesn't make us look like idiots," said Parker.

"It's either this or private school!" I climbed onto Nick's back while Parker anxiously shifted from foot to foot.

"Then what am *I* supposed to do?" he asked.

"A cartwheel!" I shouted as Nick ran into the room with me on his back.

For a moment, it was pure chaos as I whooped and punched my fist into the air. Thankfully, the class loved it and got even louder, whistling and cheering. When Nick spun around so we could watch Parker, I saw why.

My muscle-deprived wimp of a brother had his legs kicked up into the air and was *walking on his hands.*

Parker made it halfway across the room before he lost his balance and dropped back onto his feet. When he stood, his face was bright red and his hair was fluffier than ever, but he looked pleased.

I elbowed him. "I didn't know you could walk on your hands!"

"I can't. That was a cartwheel," he said.

Ms. Success closed the classroom door and motioned for everyone to quiet down. When the applause stopped, she turned to my brothers and me.

"Wow. I have not seen a room *this* excited since my karaoke performance of Lady Gaga." She cleared her throat. "Downloads of that are on my website, by the way."

She then positioned my brothers and me side by side and introduced us to the class.

"All righty. Here we have Nick, Parker, and Alexis." She touched each of our heads in turn. "Learn their names and teach them yours." She pointed to us. "I expect you to know your classmates by the end of the lesson."

"Today?" I asked, glancing at the eighteen faces watching us.

Ms. Success addressed the rest of the class. "Champs, why would I want them to know your names so quickly?"

She let her eyes wander the room and fired a finger gun at a girl with her hand raised.

"Why, Jules?"

"Because a person's name is the most important thing you can learn about them," recited Jules.

"Exactly. People love to hear—" Ms. Success stopped when Parker waved a hand to catch her attention.

"Oh, come *on*," Nick said with a groan.

Ms. Success nodded to Parker. "Something you'd like to add, Mr. Evins?"

"I don't think a person's name is the most *important* thing you can learn," said Parker. "I mean, what if they have leprosy? Wouldn't you want to know *that* first?"

Several kids in the class laughed, but Ms. Success quieted them by lifting a finger.

"Fine," she gave him a tight smile. "When it comes to meeting *most* people, nothing is as important as remembering their name."

At her command, the kids in the class introduced themselves, and I did my best to listen closely. Chloe was easy and I could remember Trevor, sitting in the back, but all the other faces were a blur. Everyone wore matching Champs shirts so I couldn't even connect the kids to unique wardrobes. Unless . . .

I reached behind me, feeling the rubberized letters of my name on my Champs shirt.

"I want to sit in the back of the room!" I blurted out as the last boy introduced himself. "I've got a . . . a fear of sitting in the front."

"Oh, Alexis." Emily, who'd been blessedly quiet, stepped forward and squeezed my arm. "You shouldn't be afraid. I'll be right here with you."

"Awww." I smiled at her, then turned again to Ms. Success. "Please!"

"It's true," spoke up Parker. "She's got . . . triskaidekaphobia."

"Yeah, she starts hyperventilating," Nick added.

I nodded, shocked that my brothers hadn't tried to call me out.

"Just a second." Ms. Success grunted and stepped away to get her seating chart.

I sidled closer to Parker. "What is triska . . . *what* do I have?" I whispered.

"The fear of the number thirteen," he answered with a grin.

Ms. Success returned, pen and chart in hand, shaking her head. "You kids today are so soft. When *I* was your age, the only things I feared were war and my Aunt Betty's parrot."

"Her parrot?" asked Nick. "Because it was mean?"

"No, because it was dead." Ms. Success scribbled on the chart. "I played with that thing for hours before anyone told me."

"Oh," said Nick, looking as disgusted as Parker and me.

Ms. Success shook her head. "I should have guessed after I tossed him in the air and he wouldn't fly. But when he hit the dirt, I just figured he was really full of birdseed."

"Okay, that *is* disturbing," I spoke up before she could continue. "But I'm glad you, uh, survived."

Ms. Success grinned and waved me away. "Go on, you. Take a seat next to Trevor."

I hurried to the back before she could change her mind,

and dropped my stuff on the desk beside Trevor's. I let out a sigh of relief. From where I was sitting, I could see the names on everyone's shirts.

"Hey." Trevor leaned toward me. "Trevor the Clever."

I just blinked at him. "Alex the Confused."

Trevor laughed and pulled away. "I meant my nickname. It's a mnemonic device. You know, something to help you remember. I've got one for everyone in the class."

I laughed too. "Oh! That *is* clever, uh, Trevor. But I knew about you even before I got here. A couple of kids from my school have a crush on you."

As soon as I'd said the words, I knew I'd broken the Holy Code of Girl. "I mean, uh, not crush. They just think you're cute." I bit my tongue. "Or maybe not even *cute*. Just not ugly."

I turned away and craned my neck to see if the seat next to Emily was still free.

"Wow. Some girls think I'm not ugly," said Trevor. "I guess I'll take that as a compliment. What school do you go to?"

I jumped on the opportunity to change the subject. "Weber, the one near the paintball course."

His face lit up. "I love paintball! Does anyone ever—"

"Trevor! Alexis!" barked Ms. Success. "Don't make me strain my singing voice."

Trevor and I stopped talking, and I put my backpack under my desk. He glanced around and whispered. "So if you go to Weber, it must be Emily and Chloe who like me, huh?"

And we were back on *that*. I smiled and put a finger to my lips. Then I leaned forward and listened as Ms. Success talked about teamwork.

"Nobody can tackle every challenge alone," she said. "Try moving furniture by yourself. Or building a house. Try choosing a new exotic pet to cheer up your aunt." She shook her head. "For the record, monkeys are a *bad* idea."

I exchanged a mystified look with Trevor, and the rest of the class buzzed with confusion until Ms. Success clapped her hands.

"The point is . . . all of those tasks are made easier when you have help." She glanced across the room and frowned. "Unless you're partnered with someone eating their own hair and looking out the window."

Everyone followed Ms. Success's gaze to a blonde girl in the far corner who seemed to be mentally miles away.

Ms. Success cupped her hands over her mouth and called to her. "Come back to us, Shelly. Your parents are paying good money for that star T-shirt."

When Shelly realized we were all watching, she let her

hair fall from her mouth and straightened up to face the front of the class.

"Now," said Ms. Success. "Teamwork . . ."

The lesson continued for half an hour until it was time to break. As we followed the rest of the class outside, Trevor pointed out the tricks he used to remember their names. Meanwhile, my brothers did what they did best and mingled with the other students. Parker made the guys laugh and Nick made the girls blush. Even Chloe.

For my sake, I really hoped she'd fall for Nick and forget all about Trevor. That way, there'd be no drama between her and Emily. Unfortunately, Chloe sauntered over to Trevor and me as soon as she spotted us.

"Hey, guys! I'm not interrupting anything, am I?" She smiled at both of us but her eyes quickly flitted to me.

"Nope," I said. "Just discussing teamwork and how great it is."

"Excellent!" Chloe scooted onto the bench between Trevor and me. "What are you doing for your teamwork assignment?"

Before I could answer, she groaned and shifted back to her feet.

"Emily the Strange is coming. I'll talk to you guys later." She leaned toward me and mumbled, "If you join an *interesting* group, let me know."

I nodded and Chloe waved to Trevor before sprinting away. Emily glanced after her, shrugged, and held a white paper bag out to Trevor and me.

"Want some? I made them myself."

She opened the bag and revealed a bunch of wrapped candies smelling strongly of chocolate.

"Yum!" I grabbed a couple and so did Trevor.

"Thanks, Emily!" he said.

I popped one into my mouth, chewed, and then stopped. It wasn't just chocolate. It was chocolate-covered *cheese*. I tried not to breathe through my nose as I swallowed.

"What do you think?" asked Emily, bouncing on her toes. "I call them 'cheesocolates.'"

Ordinarily I might have said something sarcastic, but she looked so hopeful.

"Mmmm." I rubbed my stomach. "Unique."

Trevor swallowed hard and gave her a thumbs-up. "Where'd you find the recipe?"

She blushed. "Actually, I got the idea from you."

I groaned, remembering Project Trevor.

"From me?" he asked.

"I've seen you eat Cheetos dipped in pudding," explained Emily. "I figured you must like the contrast of salty and sweet so I thought I'd make it more portable." She thrust the bag at us. "Here. Take some more!"

Trevor and I didn't budge.

"Maybe you should save those," I said. "You know, for a special occasion."

Emily waved the thought away. "Go ahead. I'm making more for Chloe's slumber party."

"Really?" I raised my eyebrows and Emily frowned. "I mean, does the world really . . . deserve them?"

"I have an idea," said Trevor. "My mom's a chef and I help her in the kitchen sometimes. Why don't we *all* make some desserts?"

Emily's face brightened and she turned to me with a pleading look. "Yes! It could be your teamwork assignment!"

Even though I imagined at least a dozen ways this could end badly, I sighed and nodded. "All right."

"Great!" Emily hugged me, then advanced on Trevor, who was too busy pawing through her candy to notice.

Before she could hug-attack him, I yanked her away by the back of her shirt and shook my head. Trevor glanced up just as Emily was smoothing her top down. "So, um, we'll meet at my place tomorrow evening?" she asked.

"Sounds like a plan!" he said.

We followed the crowd back inside for the rest of our lesson. When it was finally winding down, Ms. Success called my brothers and me to the front, and I silently recited my mnemonics so I wouldn't forget them.

Shy Shelly, B.O. Bobby, Tan Dan . . .

"All right, Evinses." Ms. Success rubbed her hands together. "You've met your classmates. I want you to point them out and tell me one thing about each of them."

My thoughts came to a grinding halt and I turned to Ms. Success. "I thought we just had to learn *names*."

Ms. Success wagged a finger. "I said I expected you to *know* your classmates, Alexis. Why don't you go first?"

There was no way I could say what I knew about each person. All of Trevor's mnemonics had been helpful but not particularly insightful. I couldn't say Dan spent too much time in the sun or that Bobby smelled like an armpit.

"Uh," I said and pointed to Shelly. "That's Shelly. She has blonde hair."

"And?" prompted Ms. Success.

I stared at Shelly's desk for clues. "Well, she's not afraid to use pens." I held up a finger. "Which is saying something because the pen is *mightier* than the sword." I paused. "That also means she's probably not afraid of swords, so if you were going into medieval battle—"

Ms. Success closed her eyes. "Move it along, Alexis."

"Right." I blushed. "Next to Shelly is Jules," I said. "She likes to wear, um, jewels. Probably diamonds, since they're a girl's best friend. As are dogs." I frowned. "Oh, wait. Dogs are a *man's* best friend. So maybe cats—"

Nick leaned over. "Stop babbling."

I struggled through the rest of the names and facts and then Parker went, followed by Nick. And, of course, they both brilliantly rattled off the names and different facts for each student.

"Well done," said Ms. Success, sending us back to our seats. "Class, your assignment that is due next lesson is teamwork. Keep it fun and keep it legal."

With a wave, she turned her back to the crowd, and there was an instant shuffling of papers and scraping of chairs as the class gathered their things to leave. My brothers and I hadn't even stepped away from our desks when Ms. Success called our names.

"Come join me for a quick powwow," she said.

"Great," muttered Parker. "I wonder what *this* could be about." He gave me a pointed look and I shoved him.

All Nick had to do was extend his massive hand, one toward each of us, and Parker and I fell silent.

As soon as everyone else had left, Ms. Success gestured for us to grab the desks closest to her.

"I'm not an idiot, kids," she said. "I know Alexis doesn't have a fear of the front of the room, and frankly, I'm offended that you'd try and stump me with triskaidekapho-bia. Nobody is afraid of snack crackers, Triscuits or other-wise."

Parker opened his mouth but then clamped it shut and nodded.

Ms. Success continued. "Alexis, I'm disappointed that you didn't try harder to get to know your classmates, *especially* since you're struggling with social skills."

I stared at my hands. "Sorry, Ms. Success."

"Work on it." She moved on to my brothers. "Nick, I didn't hear you participate once in class. Did you even read the chapters?"

"I, uh." He stuttered for a moment, then said, "I didn't have time."

Ms. Success didn't look remotely sympathetic. "Set a schedule and find some time for reading, okay?"

"Yes, ma'am."

"And Parker," she said, "I'm lethal with a high heel. If you interrupt me during class again, I'm not above decapitating you with a Jimmy Choo."

Parker nodded. "Yes, Ms. Success."

"Those things being said"—she faced us and allowed herself a small smile—"I was impressed with your over-the-top entrance. You rolled with the punches and became the Energetic Evins. You were also supportive of each other, which, I understand from your father, doesn't happen a lot." She flashed us a thumbs-up. "Keep up the good work."

We grabbed our things and headed for the exit. As

soon as we reached open air, Parker gave an all-over body shudder.

"That woman is *intense*. I think my hair's standing more on end than usual."

"And where am I supposed to find more time?" asked Nick, yawning. "I can barely stay awake for school as it is."

I snapped my fingers. "I know just the thing. Wait here!"

I hurried back into the building and went down the hall to the faculty lounge. I checked to make sure the coast was clear, then I poured a cup of coffee and walked toward the exit as fast as the sloshing liquid allowed.

Just outside Ms. Success's office door, I heard voices. Emily was talking to her stepmother.

"I'm not sure if he's doing it out of pity, but it's a start," said Emily. "I mean, he notices me now."

I pressed my back against the hallway wall. She was talking about Trevor. With Ms. Success. I never would have imagined the two of them in a conversation like *that*.

"If he was smart, he would have noticed you the whole time," said Ms. Success.

"He *is* smart," said Emily. "*I'm* just . . ." She paused and made an exasperated sound.

Ms. Success answered with a clucking tongue. "The next words out of your mouth better be positive ones. Nobody insults my kiddo."

I stared into the coffee cup I was holding and bit my bottom lip. Emily and Ms. Success were having a mother-daughter moment. I'd always wondered what those were like. Now I kind of wished I'd gotten to know firsthand.

When I walked past the office, they were too busy laughing together to even notice me.

Chapter 7 ✾

Of course the teamwork project wasn't just as simple as meeting at Emily's house. I was required to arrive half an hour *before* Trevor so Emily could go over the ground rules with me.

"Let me do most of the talking," she said. "And if I say something funny, laugh heartily."

"Laugh *heartily*?" I repeated. "As in, clutch my belly like Santa Claus?"

"No, do this . . ." She slapped her thigh and demonstrated an over-the-top laugh that almost looked painful.

"I've *never* laughed that hard," I said. "Even when Nick brushed his teeth with bodywash."

Emily groaned in aggravation and wandered into the kitchen.

"You know Trevor isn't expecting you to be a comedian," I said, following her. "Or anything else you aren't."

Emily checked her reflection in the toaster and applied more lip gloss. "I just want to offer something that Chloe doesn't. I want him to think I'm unique."

"Oh, you definitely are," I said.

She frowned at me. "Not unique like a circus freak, Alexis."

"Fine, but all joking aside, you *do* stand out," I said. "In an ambitious way. I can't think of anyone else who would buy ingredients for a hundred different desserts when she's only making one."

I gestured to the kitchen counters, which were covered with spices, fruits, and all kinds of other baking ingredients.

"I don't know what Trevor's planning to make," she said. "And I don't want him to think I'm unprepared."

The doorbell rang then, and Emily practically jumped out of her skin. "He's early!"

"Well, your stepmom *did* teach him time management skills," I pointed out.

Emily flashed me an annoyed look and ran to the door.

"Hey!" said Trevor when she let him in. He smiled at her and waved to me. "I hope you don't mind, but I brought the ingredients to make my mom's famous carrot cake." He gestured to the paper grocery bag in his arm.

The tiniest flicker of annoyance passed over Emily's face, but she forced a smile. "Mind? Why would I mind? I mean, it's not like there's dozens of groceries waiting in the kitchen."

She let out a laugh that was probably meant to sound casual but came out kind of crazy. To show my support, I slapped my thigh and said, "Ha!"

Trevor stared at both of us. "So the kitchen's through here?" He started down the hall, but Emily grabbed his elbow.

"Hey, let Alexis take that bag." She took it from Trevor and put it into my arms. "I wanted to show you something in the, uh, bathroom. It's that way." She pushed him in the opposite direction of the kitchen and turned back to me.

"Get rid of all the food!" she hissed. Then she hurried to join him.

I stood there for a second, holding Trevor's groceries and wondering just how I'd become Emily's lackey. Then I headed to the kitchen and gathered up armfuls of unopened ingredients, shoving them into the biggest empty space I could find—the dishwasher.

I'd just started laying out Trevor's items when I heard him and Emily approaching.

"Isn't that something?" she asked Trevor.

"Uh, yeah," he said. "I never noticed how much a flushing toilet sounds like the ocean." He gave me a strange look and I smiled.

"So what are we cooking up?" I asked.

"Oh, right. Voila!" Trevor reached into his back pocket and pulled out an index card.

He rattled off the list of ingredients while I grabbed the matching items. Or rather, while I *tried* to grab the matching items. Every time I reached for something, Emily would dart forward and snatch it away.

"Here are the carrots, Trevor!" she announced, followed by:

> *"Got the milk!"*
> *"All eggs accounted for!"*
> *"Pecans coming right up!"*

Just to throw her off, I grabbed a dog toy from the floor. Emily yanked it from me and, before she realized, presented it to Trevor.

He looked at the squeaky newspaper, smiled, and said, "Uh, maybe we can read *The Daily Growl* later."

Emily blushed and laughed. "Whoops!" Then she whirled around and fixed me with a frown. I shrugged innocently.

When it came time to start mixing the ingredients, Emily sidled up to one side of Trevor so I moved to the other.

She glanced at me and snapped her fingers. "You know what? We should *both* bring a dessert to the party."

I narrowed my eyes. "Huh?"

She nodded. "Alexis, why don't you go ahead and start one too?"

"Uh, because I can't cook," I said. "And because we're supposed to be practicing *teamwork*, remember?"

Emily crossed her arms and gave me a condescending smirk. "Oh, Alexis, don't you see? *We* are. We're working together to get twice as much accomplished."

I shook my head. "Unbelievable."

Clever Trevor sensed the girl trouble brewing and jumped in to help. "I can go between the two of you," he said, turning to me. "When I'm done helping Emily with a step, I can go over it with Alex."

Emily's smirk flattened, but Trevor couldn't see it with his back to her.

"That's okay," I said. "I'll try doing it on my own."

Emily flashed me a grateful smile and took Trevor's arm. "Let's get started."

"Uh, okay," he said, giving me a shrug.

As it turned out, cooking wasn't hard.

It was impossible.

The recipe instructed me to sift flour. When I asked Emily what sifting was, she wordlessly pointed to a huge silver cup with a crank on one side, and then went back to mooning over Trevor. I poured flour into the cup, and began turning the handle while I wandered over to watch them work. What I didn't realize was that there were holes in the bottom of the sifter for the flour to drain through.

When I looked into my cup to check the progress, it was completely empty, and my shoes, pant legs, and half of the kitchen were coated like a winter wonderland.

"Crud," I mumbled.

Trevor and Emily glanced at me, then down at my floury path.

"I was just making a trail back to my bowl," I said. "In case I got lost."

Trevor smiled. "At least we won't stick to the floor."

Emily rolled her eyes.

I gave up on sifting and dumped flour directly into the bowl, mixing it with the other ingredients. Then I checked the recipe again, which said to coat the baking pan with grease.

"Why?" I mumbled, flipping the pan upside down. "Hey guys, the instructions say to grease . . ."

Emily thrust a canister of shortening at me. "Here."

"Okay, but . . ." She turned back to Trevor before I could finish.

Making a face, I reached into the container for a giant glob of fat. I supposed that coating the outside of the pan with grease kept the cake from baking too fast or something. Just to make sure, I slathered it on extra thick and flipped the pan back over to pour in the batter. After sliding the cake into the oven, I joined Trevor and Emily.

"You guys need help?" I asked. "I'm pretty good with grease." I spun the shortening can on my index finger.

Trevor laughed and Emily took the container from me.

"We're doing fine, *thanks*." She smiled and nodded toward the back patio. "Why don't you wait outside?"

"Yeah, we're almost done here," said Trevor, sidling up beside her.

So much for teamwork. Without another word, I plodded outside and flopped onto a lawn chair.

A few minutes later, the sliding glass door opened.

"Alexis?" said Emily. "Are you upset or something?"

I squinted at her. "Where's Trevor? Shouldn't you be attached to his hip?"

"You *are* upset." Emily stepped closer. "Why? You didn't even want to be here."

"Yeah, but if I *have* to be here, I don't want to be excluded," I said. "I like Trevor too, you know."

Emily gasped, and I rolled my eyes.

"As a *friend*. I like having someone to bond with."

"You can bond with me," she said.

I sighed. "No, I can't. When you're not flirting with him, you're kissing up to a teacher. . . . Or worse, Ms. Success."

Emily crossed her arms. "Sharon and I have a healthy mother-daughter relationship. Something you wouldn't know anything about."

She might as well have slapped me.

My eyes dropped to the concrete patio, and instantly Emily abandoned her defensive mode.

"Oh no, that was *too* mean, wasn't it? I'm so sorry!" She squatted beside me and grabbed my hands. "Alexis!"

"It's no big deal," I said, shaking myself free and forcing a laugh.

Emily didn't look convinced. She just watched me and waited.

Finally I blurted, "Okay, yes, it *was* a big deal! I just get sick of how other people have these great moms who stick around. What was so wrong with me that *mine* wouldn't?"

A knot started building in my throat and I swallowed hard. Emily got to her feet and for a second, I thought I'd scared her off. But then she leaned forward and hugged me.

"There's *nothing* wrong with you," she said. "It's totally her loss."

I tried to fight back the emotions, but a few tears welled up when I returned her hug. "Thanks."

Before it became a Kleenex-fest, our mushy moment was interrupted by a high-pitched beeping that was coming from the kitchen. The faint smell of smoke drifted outside, and my stomach lurched.

Emily pulled away. "Is the cake done already?"

"No. Something's on fire," I said.

She gasped and shot upright. "Trevor!"

We sprinted into the house and almost collided with him as he ran toward us.

"Do you have a fire extinguisher?" he yelled to Emily over the smoke alarm.

"Yes, but it's somewhere in there!" She pointed to the kitchen.

"Wait here!" he shouted, and ran off.

Emily and I followed him without hesitation. She was in love, of course, and I just wanted to see the fire.

Inside the kitchen, the alarm was earsplitting and smoke poured out of the oven in thick, gray curls. As if that wasn't scary enough, there was a bright orange glow of fire in the oven.

Trevor jumped when he saw us. "I can't find the extinguisher, but it's Alex's cake!" He pointed at the flames.

"Alexis! What did you do?" Emily yelled over the smoke alarm.

"I don't know. I'm a fire magnet!" I climbed onto the counter and fumbled with the smoke detector until it got quiet.

Emily peered through the glass window in the oven door. "There's shortening all over the bottom of the pan. You started a grease fire!"

"*You* gave me the grease!" I shot back.

"It doesn't matter. Let's just put the fire out," said Trevor.

Emily nodded and turned to me. "When I open the oven door, you throw the box of baking soda on the flames, okay?"

"The box?" I asked. "But . . ."

Somewhere outside, a car door slammed. Ms. Success was home.

Emily looked up in alarm. "Just do it!"

"Okay, I'm on it!" I raced to the counter and searched among the cooking clutter for the baking soda. I couldn't find it so I grabbed a box of flour instead. "Go!"

Emily opened the oven door, and instantly smoke filled the room. The detector resumed its earsplitting shriek as I chucked the box of flour into the oven.

"No!" cried Emily just as the fire started licking at the cardboard. "You weren't supposed to throw the whole thing on there! What is *wrong* with you?"

"Well, I didn't think it made sense either!" I yelled. "But you said throw the box and you're the—"

Trevor grabbed both our arms, his eyes fixed on the oven. "You used baking soda, right?"

The way the color was draining out of his face, I was tempted to lie. "Uh, no," I stammered. "I couldn't find any so I used flour."

An expression of terror crossed Trevor's face. "Flour acts just like gasoline! Run!"

"Huh?"

He yanked Emily and me towards the door. Before we'd even reached the kitchen table, a ball of flame exploded from the open oven. The three of us screamed and hit the floor.

"Roll!" Emily cried. "Roll! Put out the fire!"

She started flopping around on the tile like a fish out of water, but I couldn't see anything burning on her clothes. I glanced down at my own and at Trevor's. After making sure we were flame-free, I sat up.

Other than an outward explosion of flour and smoke, the kitchen appeared fine. The fire in the oven had gone out, but all that remained of my carrot cake was a blackened lump.

"Emily." I coughed and poked her shoulder. "It's okay."

"Okay?!" cried Ms. Success from the doorway. "It looks like a nuclear winter in here!"

"Sharon!" Emily instantly stopped worrying about her invisible flames and jumped to her feet. "I'm so, so sorry!"

She lunged forward and hugged Ms. Success, who looked just as surprised as I had been when Emily had hugged me.

"It's all right." Ms. Success patted Emily's back. "The other kids are safe so we don't have to worry about a lawsuit." She raised an eyebrow at Trevor and me. "Do we?"

"No. And it wasn't all Emily's fault," I said. "We were working on our teamwork assignment. For Champs."

"Really?" Ms. Success gave a pleased grin and held Emily at arm's length. "Instead of going out to the dance clubs, you're here working on my assignment?"

"Yes, ma'am," said Emily.

I didn't bother adding that we weren't old enough to get into clubs.

"Fantastic! Well, get this place in order and carry on." She saluted us and walked away, whistling cheerfully.

With three people it didn't take long to return the kitchen to a pre-fallout state. Emily tackled the oven, I took care of the floors, and Trevor handled the dishes. When he went to put them in the washer, however, he stopped.

"Why are there groceries in the dish rack?" he asked.

Emily shot me a horrified glance, and I hurried over to Trevor.

"Oh, *that*," I said. "Ms. Success asked Emily to put away the groceries and we didn't have time."

Trevor sifted through the bags. "But these are all baking ingredients. You even have cream cheese for the frosting." He looked at us. "Why didn't you guys tell me you had this stuff?"

"Well, we . . . we wanted you to feel comfortable," I said, rubbing my neck. "You know the old saying, 'To make a guy feel at ease, uh, let him use his own cream cheese.'"

I laughed nervously and Emily joined in with a hearty thigh-slapping rendition. When Trevor didn't so much as crack a smile, I tried again.

"What I mean—"

"Wait!" blurted Emily. She turned to me. "I'm sorry, but I can't take another bad dairy rhyme. I'm lactose-humor intolerant."

That actually got a chuckle out of Trevor and gave Emily the strength to tell him the truth.

"Trevor, I bought all those groceries because I wanted you to be able to make something you liked," she said. "Because . . . because I like *you*."

Trevor stood there frozen for a moment before raising his eyebrows. "You do?" His confused expression cleared. "Ohhh. That explains the cheesocolates . . . I hope."

Emily bit her lip. "I know they were pretty disgusting, but I was trying to share your interests, and it was either that, or rent a Wookiee costume."

"Really?" he asked.

She nodded. "But the fur was too hot."

Trevor blushed. "I'm not sure what to say." He paused and shrugged. "I guess I don't think of you that way."

I winced for Emily, but she threw her shoulders back and smiled.

"It's fine. Let's just forget the whole thing. I've got desserts to remake." She turned before he could see her lower lip trembling.

I grabbed some groceries out of the dishwasher. "Wait, I'll help you."

She smiled gratefully at me and started sorting out what she needed. Without looking at Trevor, she said, "Trevor, you don't have to stay. You'll still get full credit for your teamwork assignment."

Emily and I both held our breaths and each other's gaze, wondering what he would do.

Trevor left the room.

Emily shrugged at me and blinked back tears. "Well, let's get started."

"I'm sorry," I told her.

She waved a dismissive hand. "It's no big deal."

I nodded. "That seems to be the theme of the day."

Without warning, an explosive noise punctured the air, and we both screamed and huddled together. Trevor appeared in the kitchen doorway holding a fire extinguisher.

"I'm back," he said. "And I'm ready to bake."

Emily didn't even bother trying to hide her smile.

❀ Chapter 8

On weeknights, take-out food was an Evins family staple, as was a shouting match to choose the restaurant. But when I got home from Emily's, I was greeted with silence and the aroma of grilled meat. I made a beeline for the kitchen, where Dad was brushing garlic butter on toast.

"You're making *dinner*?" I exclaimed.

Dad smiled and put a finger to his lips, nodding toward the living room. I poked my head into the other room and saw my brothers sprawled on the floor and snoring into the carpet.

I joined Dad at the stove. "What happened to them?"

He showed me an empty coffee pot with a thin film of liquid on the bottom.

"Nick?" I asked.

"He was pretty caffeine-powered before he conked out," said Dad. "When I came home, he'd already straightened up the pantry and the refrigerator. I'm guessing for his organization task for Champs."

I opened the pantry door. "Wow. He *was* busy in here."

"*And* my office," said Dad. "He rearranged the furniture and nailed the paintings on the wall. He even tried alphabetizing my books."

"Lucky for you, he doesn't know the alphabet," I said with a smile. "What about Parker?"

Dad pointed to a pair of sneakers by the back door. "For his physical skill, I told him he needs to be able to run three miles in thirty minutes. He got out of breath just tying his shoes."

I laughed. "So we *shouldn't* bet on him in any races."

"Don't underestimate your brother," Dad said. "I'm sure he's already dreaming up a device to make him move faster."

"Yeah, it's called a car."

It was nice hanging in the kitchen and talking with Dad, and when we couldn't get my brothers to wake up, he and I even ate together. During a lull in conversation, I asked him something that had been bugging me.

"Do you ever talk to Mom?" I tried to make it sound

casual as I cut into my steak, but Dad stopped eating and studied his plate. After a moment of silent contemplation, he wiped his mouth and looked at me.

"No."

Even though I'd been pretty sure of the answer, it still made my stomach hurt.

"Oh." I stabbed a potato extra hard. "Why not?"

Dad took a long drink of water and turned to me. "It's complicated, but trust me when I say it's better this way."

I nodded and cleared my throat. "Could I call—"

"Hey, I've got an idea!" He reached over and tweaked my nose. "You need an organization task for Champs, right?"

I blinked in confusion. "Uh, yeah."

"Why don't you take a shot at the garage?" he asked. "That's probably worth *double* credit!" He laughed and got up from the table.

I stayed in my chair, confused and irritated. Just because *he* didn't want to talk about Mom . . .

"Alex?" He smiled at me but it didn't reach his eyes. I could tell the subject was closed.

"Fine," I said, leaving my dirty plate on the table and storming out to the garage.

My brothers and I called it the Dispose-All. There were boxes and rubber tubs stacked everywhere, and a lot of items had apparently escaped their containers and started taking over the garage.

I went to work rounding everything up, and an hour later I'd returned almost all of the stray items back to their original homes. I was down to the last one . . . an oven mitt shaped like a hockey goalie's glove.

I rummaged around until I found a box marked "kitchen" and set it on Dad's workbench. When I ripped the tape off the top of the box, I pulled away a layer of packing foam to reveal photo albums.

"That's weird," I muttered.

Dad had given me several albums of pictures when Mom left, but I'd never seen these. I opened one on top with "Our First Year" written on it. The pictures inside were of my parents' wedding and trips they took. I put the album aside and reached for the one underneath.

"That's year two," said Dad from the garage doorway.

I jumped even though I didn't really have a reason to feel guilty. He strolled over and sat beside me.

"The albums you're holding lead all the way up until your birth," he said. "You, of course, have the rest."

I peered into the box at the years Dad had kept hidden in darkness. "Why aren't they all in the house?" I asked.

Dad flipped through the first year album. "Because they give me more pain than pleasure. But I didn't want to deny you and your brothers any memories you would have wanted to keep. So I offered each of you the albums relating to your lives."

"And I was the only one who took them?" The third album held baby pictures of Nick and Parker.

Dad shrugged. "I guess boys don't get as nostalgic as girls do about memories."

"Or maybe Nick and Parker felt the same way you did," I said. "It *is* hard to see her here." I closed the album. "And then to wonder why she never came back."

Dad put an arm around my shoulders and cleared his throat. I thought he was about to spout some words of wisdom, but all he said was, "I know."

We sat in silence, staring at the albums until I said, "Why did you put them in a box marked 'kitchen'?"

"Because I don't cook much," said Dad with a sheepish grin. "I figured I'd never come across them." He patted my leg. "I'd say you've completed your organization task, wouldn't you?"

"*Yes.*" I grabbed the box and glanced at him expectantly. "Is it okay—"

"You can keep the photos," he said.

I hugged him, and we went back inside to find Nick and Parker eating dinner.

"Awww. Looks like we slept through some Dispose-All fun," Nick said with a smile.

Parker shook his head. "Darn the luck."

"Let me make it up to you, boys." Dad winked at me. "Why don't the two of you start on the dishes and tomorrow, you can finish the garage?"

"Awww!" Nick said again.

I headed for my room with the photo box, but Parker yelled my name.

"Your friend Chloe called," he said, pointing at the message board. "She said it was important."

I groaned, remembering her request from Champs. *If you join an interesting group, let me know.*

I'd teamed up with Trevor and hadn't said a word.

"Did she say what she wanted?" I asked.

He shrugged. "Something about hockey boosters?"

Feeling slightly relieved, I picked up the phone and dialed, barely managing a hello before Chloe cut in.

"Ms. Success was going over your social activities and found out we were in hockey boosters together," she said in a rush. "She asked what we were working on, and . . . well, the good news is, she was impressed."

"Really? By the banners we made?" I asked.

Chloe was quiet for a second.

"Was it the extra glitter?" I asked, smiling. "Or how we rhymed 'score' with 'more'?"

"Uhhh, that's the bad news," Chloe finally said. "I didn't tell her about the banners. I kind of lied."

I stopped smiling. "What?"

Chloe's voice came out barely above a whisper. "I said we were teaching elementary school kids about hockey."

I closed my eyes and sighed. "But you don't know about hockey. You thought the goalie was an umpire."

"I know," said Chloe.

"And another girl thought the puck was a giant peppermint patty."

"I *know*," she said. "But now she wants to see the presentation we put together. Alex, we're doomed!"

I paced the kitchen floor, wishing I could reach through the phone and throttle Chloe. Of all the people to lie to, she chose the one who could send me off to private school.

"Alex?"

"Call the other hockey boosters," I said. "Make sure they can get together tomorrow for an emergency meeting during homeroom. It's time for Hockey 101."

The next morning, I showed up for the meeting decked out in hockey gear: pads, mask, and all. When I entered the room where the girls were gathered, they all stared at me.

"Chloe's missing?" I said, my voice muffled by the mask. "That's too bad. I wanted all of you here at once."

"What's . . . going on?" a girl asked nervously.

I pulled out a hockey stick and waved it at her. "I'm here to teach you a lesson."

Several of the girls looked at one another and screamed, "We're all gonna die!"

"Woah!" I held up my arms and backed away toward the door. "Wait! Not that kind of lesson!"

"She's blocking the exit!" someone shrieked. "Go out the window!"

Chloe came through the door behind me. "*What* is going on? I can hear you guys screaming out in the hallway."

"Chloe, look out!" one of the girls cried. "Alex is packing puck!"

I ripped off my mask. "Would you calm down? I just wanted to teach you about hockey."

One of the girls, who was stacking chairs by the window, stopped. "Then why are you dressed like Jason from the Halloween movies?"

I stared at her incredulously. "I'm dressed like a hockey player. You know, the sport you're all so fond of?"

The girls looked at one another and then at me.

"Just . . . sit down," I said.

While the girls settled into chairs, I brought out the posters I'd made.

"Oh, I like that one, with all the reds and blues!" said a girl who I remembered as Claire. "What is it?"

At this point, I had no idea why I was even surprised. "It's a diagram of a hockey rink," I said. "Haven't you ever been to one?"

"Well, yes, but I'm not usually checking out the ice," she said.

And then the lightbulb went on over my head.

"You're into hockey for the guys, aren't you?" I asked.

She nodded, along with several other girls.

"But we get bored quickly," said Claire. "The guys go on and off the ice, like, every two minutes."

"Yeah. As soon as you find a cute one, he's gone," another girl said. "Or he loses a tooth."

"And they're really clumsy," piped up someone else. "They keep running one another into the walls."

"You mean body checking," I said with a smile.

Then I started with the explanations. I talked about checking, the blue and red lines, and the basics of the game.

"When do they try to rope the Zamboni?" asked Claire.

I sighed. "Never. It's for smoothing out the ice."

By the time homeroom ended, the girls seemed to

understand hockey well enough to follow along with the presentation I'd put together.

"I owe you big time," said Chloe, helping me take down my posters.

"Just don't lie to Ms. Success anymore," I said.

Chloe smiled. "Deal. Speaking of Champs, what did you end up doing for your teamwork task?"

She and I stepped into the hallway, and I took my time navigating the crowd for an excuse not to answer. For some reason, I didn't think it wise to tell the whole truth, so I said, "I baked desserts with Emily for the slumber party."

"Kissing up to the teacher's assistant." Chloe elbowed me. "Clever! Not that I would have traded places with you in a hundred years." She grabbed my arm. "Then you're still coming to the slumber party?"

"That's the plan," I said.

"Great. See you at Champs tonight! I'll keep the seat by Trevor warm for you." She gave me a conspiratorial wink and strolled down the hall.

Emily poked her head around the corner of a locker bay and I let out a startled yelp.

"Chloe likes Trevor too, doesn't she?" she asked.

I sighed. "Listen, you should just let it go. Let *him* go. It's not worth the hassle."

Emily stared after Chloe. "You're probably right."

But she didn't look like she believed me.

That evening when I got to Champs, Chloe wasn't warming my seat. Instead, to my annoyance, a grungy skater chick was there, talking to Trevor.

I cleared my throat. "Um, excuse me. I just had that chair disinfected."

Trevor laughed, and the girl gave a derisive snort. "Geez, Alex. Relax!"

She caught my eye and I gasped.

Emily's perfect ponytail was gone. Her hair was now draped around her face, hanging to her shoulders . . . and she'd dyed it *black*. On top of that, her eye makeup was so thick that she'd have to peel it off in order to remove it.

"Em-Emily?" I could only stutter her name. All other words had left my vocabulary.

She smirked lazily and leaned on the desk. "That's what the kids call me."

I glanced at Trevor, who gave an amused shrug. Then I grabbed Emily's arm and pulled her toward the door. "Let's step outside for a second."

"What, the phrase 'excuse me' isn't in your vocabulary?" She rolled her eyes at Trevor.

"Just go!" I pushed Emily in front of me.

Once I'd closed the door, she gathered her hair into its usual ponytail.

"That went well, don't you think?" she asked, beaming.

I stared at her. "*What* went well? Your frontal lobotomy?"

Emily frowned. "Excuse me?"

"You've lost your mind! And your stepmother," I said as I flicked her black ponytail, "is going to kill you!"

Emily waved me away. "It's a wig, and Sharon already knows about all of this." She made a sweeping gesture from her head to her ripped jeans, and I noticed for the first time that she was wearing an Ankle Biters T-shirt.

I pointed at it and exclaimed, "You don't even like them!"

"Shhh!" Her eyes widened and she pushed me farther from the door. "Trevor doesn't know that," she said.

I marveled at her idiocy. "I'm pretty sure he'll figure it out when he plays one of their songs and you run away screaming!"

"That's not going to happen." Emily tugged on the front of her shirt, as though even *wearing* something related to the band made her uncomfortable. "Besides, sometimes sacrifices are necessary to make romance work."

"Wha—? Romance?" I dug my fingers into my hair. "Emily, this is stupid! You shouldn't have to change for *anybody*."

She crossed her arms over her chest. "Chloe likes him too. The only way I can compete with her is to be Trevor's dream girl."

"Dream? You're acting like a nightmare," I scoffed.

Emily looked dumbstruck. "For your information, I learned this behavior from *you*!" She poked me in the shoulder. Hard.

My jaw dropped, but I quickly drew it back up. "Fine. Then let me teach you something *else!*"

Before she could react, I grabbed Emily in a headlock and dragged her to the drinking fountain.

"Augh! Let go! You'll mess up my wig!" She squealed and slapped at my arms.

"We're washing that eye makeup off," I said. "If we're lucky, maybe some of your crazy will rinse away too."

Someone turned the knob of the classroom door, and I instantly released her.

"Is everything okay?" asked Trevor, stepping into the hallway. "I heard screaming."

"Everything's fine," I said. "Emily was just singing an Ankle Biters song for me." I bumped her shoulder. "Why don't you sing it for Trevor?"

Emily's face, which had been red from our struggle, turned redder still. "Oh, I don't think he wants, um . . ." She laughed nervously. "It's better with music."

He smiled and nodded toward the door. "Come on. Class is about to start."

Emily let her shoulders relax and gave a cocky half-smile, and sauntered into the classroom. I followed, searching for something large enough to knock her unconscious.

"Hello, Champs!" boomed Ms. Success as we got seated. "I hope your last few days have been almost as riveting as this interview I did." She held up a copy of *Loud Women*. "Don't let the name fool you," she said to a chorus of giggles. "People who make the most noise get the most attention."

"And the most spit in their food at restaurants," I whispered to Trevor.

He snickered into his hand, and Ms. Success whipped around to look at us.

"Alexis . . ." She pointed at me, and I knew I was busted.

"Yes, ma'am?" I said in my meekest voice.

"Our lesson today is leadership," said Ms. Success. "I understand you know a little something about that."

Everyone swiveled to look at me, including my brothers. That was *not* what I'd expected her to say.

"S-sorry?" I asked.

"The hockey boosters," said Ms. Success. "Chloe tells me you jumped right into a leadership role when you joined."

"Oh!" I hadn't thought of it that way, but I *had* taken charge of the boosters that morning.

Ms. Success gave me a thumbs-up. "I'm thrilled that my wisdom sank in so fast. Now, for the rest of you. . . ."

Trevor nudged me while Ms. Success started the lesson. "Way to go!"

"Thanks," I told him, glancing at Chloe.

She had turned partially in her chair and smiled when she saw me looking. I smiled back.

Maybe I had other girls figured out wrong. Maybe the slumber party wouldn't be so terrible. Maybe . . .

Chloe's glance drifted to Trevor. Over her shoulder, I could see Emily frowning at them both.

Maybe I needed to bring riot gear.

Chapter 9 ❀

Saturday night Dad drove me and my cake to Chloe's. Even before I got out of the car, we could hear squeals and laughter accompanied by bad, bad singing.

Dad cleared his throat. "Are you sure you want to do this?"

"Oh, yeah!" I said with way more enthusiasm than either of us found believable. "I mean, it'll be fine. I should really try this socializing thing."

He kissed my forehead. "I'm proud of you. Have fun."

Like a soldier heading into battle, I slung my duffle bag over my shoulder and steeled myself for an assault of perfume and powder puffs. For protection, I held the carrot cake straight out in front of me.

I hadn't even knocked before the door was thrown open by two girls in bathing suits and towels. They giggled and pulled me into the house.

"Get changed, Alex! Everyone's out by the pool," said Claire from hockey boosters.

"But it's almost October," I said.

"It's a *heated* pool," Claire said.

"Ooh, cake!" said the other girl, taking it from me. "Who wants a sugar rush?" she called, hurrying toward the back door with Claire.

Chloe wandered in from another room. "Hey, Alex! I'm so glad you could make it!" She took my duffle bag and motioned for me to follow her downstairs.

"Thanks again for what you did in Champs the other day," I said. "Ms. Success didn't even make me do a leadership task."

The expressions on my brothers' faces had been priceless when I told them.

Chloe waved my thanks away. "That's what friends are for. We look out for one another."

A twinge of guilt rumbled through my stomach and I tried to shake it off. Technically, I hadn't done anything wrong. I just hadn't told Chloe about one little get-together with Trevor. And since Emily was involved, Chloe probably wouldn't have even wanted to go.

I distracted myself from the feeling by taking in all the

plaques and ribbons decorating the wall of the stairwell. At the base of the stairs stood a trophy case half-filled with gold and silver cups.

"Wow. You have a lot of awards," I said.

"I like to win," she said simply. "And soon I'll have another trophy to add to my collection when we take the Champs championship." She nudged me. "Right?"

"Huh? Oh, right!" I'd forgotten our agreement to compete together. "We'll show those other 'Champs.'" I put the word in air quotes.

"Come on. We can put your stuff in the rec room," Chloe said, leading me inside. "Everyone's in the pool. It's *heated*, you know."

"So I've heard. And *everyone's* there?" I asked, ducking to avoid a row of balloons taped above the archway.

"Well almost . . ." Chloe smirked and dropped my bag in an empty corner beside a cot. The cot was covered with a pastel quilt, neatly tucked in at the corners, and a ruffled pillow embroidered with a gigantic, gold *E*.

Even without the monogrammed clue, I would have been able to guess who it belonged to. The rest of the room was wall-to-wall sleeping bags decorated with movie stars, pop stars, and Japanese cartoons.

"So where did you hide Emily?" I unrolled my black sleeping bag beside her cot.

Chloe shrugged. "She didn't want to practice dance moves with us so I told her she could do something else. She's in the kitchen setting out the snacks my mom bought."

"Oh." I frowned. "That doesn't sound like fun. You didn't try to convince her to go outside?"

"What can I say? Good help is hard to find." Chloe grinned at me.

This time I felt a different twinge: irritation.

"Oh, and I have something for you!" Chloe skipped across the room and pulled a small plastic bag out from under a furry, pink pillow. "Your Emily-taming tools."

"My what?" I peeked in at the contents of the bag: earplugs, a laser pointer, a blank CD, and twenty dollars.

Something else I'd forgotten about. "Uh, thanks," I said, pocketing the twenty and putting the bag under my own pillow. Now that I was getting along with Emily, the bag seemed kind of embarrassing. "I think I'll go check on her now."

"Ah, good thinking." Chloe winked at me. "Make sure she isn't adding any last-minute 'special ingredients' to the food." She mimed choking and dying.

I faked a laugh that turned into a grumble as soon as I was out of earshot. In the kitchen, Emily was flitting around a long table wrapped in colorful plastic vinyl.

"You're the life of the party, huh?" I asked.

"Take the lid off that potato salad," she said by way of answer. "And where's your dessert?"

"Being devoured poolside. Why didn't you want to practice dance moves?" I asked. "Not that I blame you."

"Oh, I got the moves down after the second try." Emily swished the end of her ponytail over her shoulder. "Then I got bored watching everyone else flail around."

"You couldn't have stayed just to socialize?" I asked.

As soon as I heard my own words, I froze. Just a few days ago, my role had been reversed with Emily's, and *she* was trying to convince *me* to be the social butterfly. Was I being brainwashed, Champs-style?

Emily didn't notice. "I know it seems like I should be out there, given that I don't have many friends—"

"That's not true. You have lots of friends," I said.

Emily narrowed her eyes at me. "I'm not a moron. I get that my personality can be a little hard to bear."

"Oh. Then go on."

"I've got a good friend," she said, pointing to me, "*most* of the time. And I have a romantic interest. I don't need anything else." Emily clasped her hands together and looked thoughtful. "Live simply. That's my new philosophy."

"Okay. Well, I have a different philosophy." I tugged her toward the door. "If I have to suffer, you have to suffer."

We stepped into the backyard and were almost soaked by

two girls holding buckets of water. At the very last second, they saw Emily and jerked back so that only a little water sloshed onto the grass.

"Sorry," said one of the girls. "We thought Alex was alone."

"That was meant for *me*?" I asked, not sure whether to feel angry or included.

"We wanted to . . . *persuade* you to get into your bathing suit," said one of the bucket holders.

"Saying 'please' works too," I said, "unless I'm on fire."

Then a brilliant idea popped into my head.

"Speaking of fires," I pulled Emily onto a lounge chair with me, "you would never believe what happened to us on Wednesday. Hollywood should be calling to make Emily and I stuntwomen."

I now had the attention of every girl within hearing distance.

"What happened?" someone asked.

"Well . . . Emily, you should tell it." I pushed her toward the crowd. "It happened at your house anyway."

"Huh?" At first, Emily just fixed me with an incredulous stare, but when she noticed all eyes on her, she started talking.

"Okay, so we, uh, we decided to make desserts for the party, and I bought all these ingredients," she said, chewing her lip. "Looking back, I probably should have bought a fire hose too."

Several girls laughed at her unintended joke, and Emily smiled and continued. I noticed that she was as careful as I'd been not to mention Trevor's involvement in the adventure. I relaxed a little, realizing she didn't want a fight with Chloe any more than I did.

As her story went on, the crowd grew closer and quieter, so that when Emily got to the part where we tried to put the fire out, each girl in the backyard was hanging on her every word.

"Alexis threw flour into the oven, thinking it would smother the flames, but what she didn't know"—Emily leaned toward her audience and whispered—"is that flour acts just . . . like . . . gasoline."

"Oh, no!" Someone gasped.

"You're lucky to be alive!" said someone else.

"We would've been toast," I added, getting into the spirit of things, "if it hadn't been for Trevor."

I realized my mistake too late and clamped my mouth shut. Emily stiffened, but didn't dare look at me.

"Who's Trevor?" asked Claire.

"Just a guy," I said.

"Oooh, a *guy*." She winked, *not* helping the situation.

"So, you were hanging out with him?" Chloe's voice,

sounding sharp, came from over my shoulder. "Doing your teamwork task?"

I turned to face her. "It wasn't a big deal."

Emily chimed in. "He overheard Alexis and I talking about the desserts we were making for your party and offered to help." She smiled broadly at Chloe, challenging her to press the issue.

Not a single splash came from the pool as the other girls watched the silent showdown. Finally, Chloe laughed and gave me a friendly slap on the arm. It was meant to *look* friendly, at least.

"I was just curious. No biggie!"

The other girls relaxed and Emily went back to the story. The rest of the evening proceeded with pillow fights and gossip sessions. By the time we all laid down for the night, Chloe seemed to have completely forgotten the incident.

Or at least I thought she had.

Shortly before dawn, I jolted awake, unable to breathe. Chloe had one hand over my mouth and the other pinching my nostrils shut. It was probably meant to scare me, but since I'd grown up sparring with my brothers, I simply shoved her away.

"*What* is your problem?" I hissed in my quietest voice.

She put a finger to her mouth and nodded toward the

staircase. I followed her to the back porch, and as soon as she'd closed the doors behind her, she exploded with fury.

"Trevor is off-limits!" she snapped. "What part of that did you not get the *first* time?"

"Seriously?" I groaned and rubbed my eyes. "I can't believe you woke me up for this. I'm going back to sleep."

"No, you're not! We're not done!" She grabbed my arm and yanked me off-balance.

Now I was starting to remember why I didn't hang out with other girls.

"Chloe," I said, doing my best to stay calm, "you're over-reacting. Let's talk later."

"You think I'm overreacting?" she squeaked. "You just stole the love of my life!"

I rolled my eyes up to the heavens. "If you're so in love with him, what's his favorite type of movie?"

"Movie?" Chloe paused in her rampage. "Um . . ."

"Sci-fi," I said. "What does he dip Cheetos in?"

She tugged on the drawstrings of her pajama bottoms. "Ranch dressing?"

"Chocolate pudding," I said. "If you're really so concerned that I'm trying to steal him, maybe you should try harder to keep his attention."

After hearing my logic, a sane person would have nodded and been embarrassed. Since Chloe was an irrational psycho, however, she went ballistic.

"You *are* trying to take him from me! I knew it!" She charged at me, arms flying.

Over the past week, I'd made a serious effort to be friendly, and social, and play the part of an average girl, but even the average girl had her limits.

So I stepped aside and let Chloe fall into the pool.

It was blissfully quiet for the five seconds she flailed around underwater, but as soon as her head broke the surface, she made sure everyone in a two-block radius knew her anguish.

"Aughhh!" she screamed, pounding the water with her fists.

I crouched by the edge of the pool, just beyond her reach. "I'm only going to say this once more. I . . . don't . . . like . . . Trevor."

Chloe growled and lunged at me, but since she was water-logged, it was more of a slow-motion belly flop.

From the direction of the house came the sound of the doors bursting open, followed by a familiar gasp.

"Alexis!" cried Emily, running toward me. "You pushed Chloe in?"

"No," I said. "She fell in before I had the chance."

Emily clapped her hand to her forehead.

"Relax," I said with a smile. "It's a *heated* pool."

Emily gripped my shoulders. "You have to do major damage control *right now!*" She glanced behind her where girls were streaming out the back door to see what had happened.

"Okay," I said.

Then I pushed Emily into the pool.

Several of the closest girls gasped and I turned to face them.

"Pajama pool party!" I shouted, and did a backflip into the deep end.

Even submerged I could hear the giggles and feel the splashes around me as everyone joined in. When I reached open air, I came face-to-face with Emily, who tried to scowl at me but burst out laughing. Everyone was having a great time except, of course, Chloe, who was staring murderously at me. I almost expected the water around her to start boiling over from her anger.

And then someone said, "Chloe, this was an *awesome* idea!"

"So fun!" another girl agreed. "The best slumber party this year."

All the other girls chorused their agreement and instantly Chloe's bad humor vanished. After we'd all dried off later, I expected her to confront me again, but she didn't say another word on the subject. And when Dad came to pick me up, she simply thanked me for coming.

Part of me was relieved that she'd finally gotten my point, but another part of me wondered if the pool incident had given her a new reason to hate me.

Chapter 10 ✻

I have to say, I'm impressed." Dad tossed my
duffle bag in the backseat while I carried a party tin
of cheese popcorn. "I didn't get a call in the middle
of the night saying you'd put someone in the hospital or the
trunk of a car."

"That's because I'm a perfect angel," I said with my most
innocent expression.

Dad laughed and put the car in gear. "I would never
believe *that*, but I'm glad everything turned out okay. Did
you have fun?"

"Yep," I said.

"Enough to go again?" he asked with a grin.

"Nope." I smiled back. "How are Nick and Parker

doing? Did they have a good time without me?"

"Well, Nick spent the evening with a tutor and Parker spent it running the track."

"In other words, no." I made a face. "What are they doing now?"

"Parker is supposed to be helping Nick study," said Dad. "Although I'm not sure how well that's going."

"Nick?" I turned toward him. "You're joking."

Dad shook his head. "He's been taking this Champs business pretty seriously."

"Well, I'd hate to interrupt *that*," I said. "I guess if they're busy I'll just relax in my room."

"Sure," said Dad. "You've earned it."

I wondered if he'd feel the same if he knew what had really happened at Chloe's, but all I said was, "Thanks."

Back at the house, I shouted a hello to my brothers, who were taking a break in the kitchen, and ran up to my room. Dad never liked us to lock our doors, but I figured I could get away with it for half an hour or so.

Pushing aside a pile of laundry in my closet, I pulled out the box of photos from the garage and carried it to my bed. I flipped through the first three albums that I'd already seen, but took my time once I got to the newer ones.

I was hoping I'd be able to understand Mom better if I could peek into her past, but the more I saw, the more confused I became. There would be several pictures of her awkwardly posed with my brothers, face devoid of any emotion, and then there would be a picture of her clutching her pregnant belly and smiling, as if she was thrilled to be a mom.

I compared them to the albums I had from after I was born and it was the same pattern. I'd be sitting on the floor by Mom's desk while she worked, completely ignoring me, and later I'd be sitting on her lap while she pointed out pictures in one of her books.

There was a loud thud outside my bedroom door and I quickly fumbled to put the albums back in the box. A couple of photos fell out of their sleeves, and I scooped them up, hiding them behind my back as I crept to my door to listen. When I didn't hear anything else, I climbed back onto the bed and set to work replacing the fallen photos.

Except, behind one of them, someone had tucked in a note.

I pulled it out and recognized the same handwriting that I'd seen on so many birthday and Christmas checks—Mom's.

Despite your wishes (and angry letters),
I will continue to send money to OUR
children. I know you refuse to believe
me, but I'm incredibly disappointed
the meeting with the boys didn't go as

*planned. It may be too much to ask, but
please help them to understand. Give the
boys and Alexis my love (and keep a
little for yourself).*

I stared at the note in disbelief. I re-read it. Then I flipped it over but there was no date on it. I read it one more time, but it was getting harder to focus on the words with the note shaking in my hand. Several thoughts struggled to be first in my mind.

Mom loved us . . . or she had at some point, anyway.
Mom had met with my brothers, but not me.
Dad had tried to cut off communication with Mom,
even birthday checks.

But why?

The knob on my bedroom door jiggled and I leapt about a foot into the air.

"Alex?" Dad's muffled voice carried through the door. "Are you decent?"

"Uh, yeah!" I threw a blanket over the box and shoved the note in my back pocket. I wasn't quite ready to share it with anyone. "Just a sec."

I took a few deep breaths and then opened the door. "Sorry. I just wanted a little private time."

Dad nodded. "I'm heading out to the grocery store. Apparently, exercise is turning Parker into a bit of an eating machine."

"He gets full after a carrot stick," I said. "How much can he eat?"

Dad crossed his arms. "Well, the refrigerator's almost empty, and if metal was edible, I'm sure he would have swallowed *that*, too."

I laughed. "Yeah, okay."

"Just be on your guard," said Dad. "And don't wear any food costumes."

I pushed him and laughed again. He disappeared down the hall and I leaned against the door frame. Dad was usually so patient and good-humored. What could Mom have done to set him off? I returned to the box of photo albums and started poking behind all the photo sleeves, looking for more notes. Unfortunately, it seemed that this was the only one to have made its way into the box.

I heard more thumping outside my door, followed by an assortment of odd grunts. After shoving the box under my bed, I poked my head into the hallway.

"*What* are you guys doing?"

My brothers were sprawled out on the carpet of the second-story landing, Parker fighting to break free from Nick, who had him in a headlock.

"Give it here!" Nick shouted, reaching for something Parker had clutched in his fist.

"Never!" Parker twisted his hand out of reach and brought whatever he was holding to his mouth.

Nick looked up at me. "Alex! Stop him!"

I dropped down between the two of them and clawed at Parker's hand. "What is it? Parker, let . . . ugh!"

Whatever it was smushed between my fingers as I grabbed for it, and I recoiled in horror. My hand was coated in reddish-brown ooze.

"Nooo!" cried Parker.

"Please tell me this didn't come from someone's nose." I wiped my fingers on Parker's shirt.

"It *was* a moldy strawberry he found in the back of the refrigerator," said Nick, releasing Parker from his grip.

"What?!" I stared at my brother in disgust.

"I was going to eat *around* the mold." Parker glanced hungrily down at his shirt where I'd wiped my hand.

"Don't even think about it," said Nick.

"But I'm starving!" cried Parker.

"Dad'll be home soon with more groceries," I said. "Why don't you go back to whatever you were doing before this?"

Nick snorted. "He wasn't doing anything. He was *supposed* to be helping me study for a test tomorrow since my tutor isn't working out."

"You've only had one session," I said. "How can you already know that?"

"I thought I'd get one of those cute, smart girls for my tutor, like how it always works on sitcoms," said Nick.

"Yes. Because our lives are so laugh-a-minute," said Parker, getting to his feet and heading for the bathroom.

"Anyway," Nick said, "I wound up with this guy from Dad's college. All he did was babble about geometry, and all I did was count the hairs curling out of his nose."

"So you did do *some* math," I said with a smile.

"Well, I'm sorry," said Parker from the bathroom doorway, "but I can't help you study on an empty stomach. All this exercise is making me hungry." He uncapped a tube of toothpaste and squeezed the contents into his mouth.

"Parker!" I jumped up and knocked the toothpaste out of his hand while Nick forced his head into the sink.

Begrudgingly, Parker spit out the toothpaste and turned to glare at us. "You're lucky I didn't bite off a few fingers." Parker's eyes lit up. "Ooh. Chicken fingers!"

Nick looked ready to pummel him so I stepped between my brothers. "Wait! I have a big tin of cheese popcorn."

"*Really?*" Sheer joy shone on Parker's face, but it was quickly replaced by annoyance. "Were you going to tell me before or *after* I ate rotten fruit and toothpaste?"

I stuck my tongue out at him. "The deal is this: Help

Nick study, and you can have a handful of popcorn for every answer he gets right."

"But then I'll never eat again!" moaned Parker.

"Hey!" Nick frowned. "I'm not *that* hopeless."

"And *you*"—I pointed at Nick—"have to at least try, with or without his help. Agreed?"

Nick and Parker glowered at each other.

"Agreed," they said in unison.

I grabbed the tin of popcorn from my room and handed it to Nick. I couldn't put it past Parker to push me down the stairs for it.

"To the living room," I said.

While my brothers studied, I watched them and thought about the note in my back pocket. I didn't find it difficult to believe that something had gone wrong at their meeting with Mom, but I did have trouble believing *I* hadn't been invited. Or that I hadn't at least been told about it. I wanted to ask while Dad wasn't around, but I couldn't take away Nick's study time.

The front door opened, and Dad appeared with an armful of paper bags. My brothers glanced up, but Parker didn't leap over the couch to get to the groceries. He simply nodded at Dad and grabbed a handful of popcorn as Nick correctly solved an equation.

"Glad to see the house is still standing," Dad said as I took some bags from him. "Did I miss something?"

"Why would you think that?" I asked, leading the way to the kitchen.

"Your brothers aren't fighting over that popcorn tin, and they're actually working together. Did you have something to do with that?"

I smirked at him. "If I did, I'm very clever. Wouldn't you say?"

In answer, Dad kissed my forehead. "I'm proud of you. A few weeks ago, you wouldn't have done anything to help," he said. "Or you would have buried the popcorn in the backyard and given Parker a treasure map."

I tilted my head to one side thoughtfully. "Yeah. I was a lot more fun a few weeks ago."

The next morning, on the way to school, I shared Mom's note with Emily. After her eyebrows had returned to their normal position, she asked, "How old do you think this is?"

I shrugged. "It can't be too recent because my dad would still be upset. I'm thinking it has to be at least a few years old."

"And all this time, your mom's probably been thinking of you."

I didn't answer Emily. It was a strange feeling to think

Mom might be gazing out a window somewhere, wondering what we were up to. I'd always assumed we were just a mark on the calendar when it was time to mail off checks.

"You have to try and get in touch with her," said Emily.

I folded the note and put it back into my pocket. "I'm not sure that's a good idea."

Emily stopped me. "You can't be serious. All this time, you've been upset about your mom. Now you know she's out there and that your brothers have had communication with her. . . ."

"I know," I said. "But they obviously stopped talking for some reason, and I don't want to be the one to reopen old wounds."

"But aren't you even the least bit curious?" pressed Emily. "Don't you want to find out what happened when she met your brothers and, more important, why she didn't meet you?"

I frowned. "You're a bad influence, you know that?"

Emily rolled her eyes. "I'm just saying. . . . You have the chance to bring your family together again. Don't just write it off."

I shook my head. "I'll think about it. Let's change the subject."

Emily cleared her throat and casually glanced at her nails. "You mean, to how Trevor and I played paintball yesterday?"

I gasped. "What?! You didn't."

"We did!" Emily dropped the nonchalant act and bounced up and down. "He called Saturday night while we were at Chloe's, and when I called him back yesterday, he said he'd been thinking about how I liked him."

"And?"

"And he thought I was odd but sweet." She blushed.

I smiled. Only Emily would take that as a compliment.

"So you know the cheese popcorn everyone got as a party favor from Chloe?" she went on. "I asked if he wanted something new to try with pudding."

"Clever!" I said.

"He came over and realized that I live near the paintball course."

"And, of course, you just *love* paintball," I said, grinning.

"I do now," she said. "It was so much fun, and look!" She rolled up her sleeve to reveal a purple bruise on her arm. "Trevor did that with a paintball." With the way she smiled, anyone would have thought he'd tattooed his name there. "We're going out again next Friday."

"Awww. That's great," I said. "And will you serve pudding at the wedding?"

She smirked and rolled her sleeve down. "Funny. But we haven't told anyone we've started dating yet just in case of you-know-who."

I raised an eyebrow. "You're not really scared of Chloe,

are you? From what I hear about your power at school, she should be afraid of *you*."

Emily drew herself up, looking offended. "I'm not scared of *anybody*, but if a girl like that gets upset, she can be dangerous. I think you know what I mean." Emily gave me a pointed look.

"True."

"And with me being the Champs assistant and him being a student, Chloe could say I'm favoring him *or* that my stepmom's favoring him."

"Got it," I said, zipping my lips together. "I won't say a thing."

She smiled gratefully. "And while we're on Chloe, have you talked to her at all?"

"Since I introduced her to sleepwear swimming?" I shook my head. "I don't think she'll be speaking to me again any time soon."

But I was wrong.

During PE, when everyone lined up for badminton, Chloe chose a spot behind me.

"Hey," she said with a forced smile.

"How's it going?" I asked.

"Well, I'm not in wet pajamas, so pretty good," she said. "What about you? Been causing trouble?" She crossed her arms and glared at me. "Or is that something you save for parties?"

I groaned. "You really want to do this now?" When she didn't answer, I sighed. "Look, I'm sorry you fell in the pool, but everything turned out okay."

"Lucky for you," she snapped. "The only reason I haven't told everyone you pushed me—"

I held up my hands. "Wait. I didn't push you."

Her lip curled maliciously. "In *my* version of the story, you did."

It was my turn to cross my arms. "And how many people have heard *your* version?"

"Nobody . . . yet. But only because I need you on my team to win the Champs Championship *and* to get Trevor."

"Trevor?" I repeated.

"He agreed to join only if you would," she said bitterly.

"Smart guy," I said. "I'm not sure I'd want to be alone with you either."

Anger sparked in Chloe's eyes. "Trevor and I will be spending a *lot* of time together. So much, in fact, he won't be able to help but fall for me."

I raised an eyebrow. "And have you been practicing an evil laugh to go with that plan of yours?"

She narrowed her eyes. "If you don't help me win this contest, Alex, you'll see just how evil I can get."

❀ Chapter 11

I didn't have much time to focus on Chloe's threat. I was too busy thinking about Mom's note and keeping up with schoolwork, Champs, and the hockey boosters.

I even took the boosters to a high school match on Wednesday. Of course, I had to make it the *girl's* team so they'd pay attention to the actual game, but they stayed in their seats even after they ran out of hot chocolate. And seeing how interested the boosters were gave me a great idea to have a hockey scrimmage to raise money for the Champs Championship.

That week's Champs lessons were on confidence and goal-setting, and at the end of class on Thursday, Ms. Success made an announcement.

"As you all know and should be eagerly awaiting, the Champs Championship is two weekends from now."

She paused while the class clapped and cheered.

"I'm hoping you'll make your parents *and* me proud." She continued, "But mainly me because I've got a documentary on the line." She nodded to Emily, who handed out a stack of papers. "By the way, I need all of your parents to sign these filming waivers."

While everyone read the paperwork, she walked up and down the aisles.

"Today you'll sign up for teams, and no." She held up a hand. "I can't join you, but thank you for asking."

She leaned against the window. "I'm an impartial judge, and I want *all* of my students to win. I can't be bought with chocolates or fruit baskets. Mainly because I don't like them, but also because they're wrong."

"Are gift certificates wrong?" someone asked.

The class laughed, and Ms. Success chuckled and wagged a finger. "Depends on the amount." She turned to the rest of us. "Now, if all of you remember, to compete in the championship, you must first raise the money. On . . . your . . . own."

She frowned to show she was serious. "The fund-raising is an opportunity to utilize all the skills you've learned in this class. It's also the one time I will not accept money from your parents. You *must* earn this. Understood?"

We all nodded, and she clapped her hands together. "Then let's assemble in teams of three."

While everyone else scurried about, I kept my seat, uncertain of what to do. I needed a team obviously, but I wasn't sure if I should suffer the pain of being with Chloe or try and force myself in with strangers. The only trouble was, everyone else seemed to have already established a group.

As I was starting to feel a little sorry for myself, a ball of paper flew through the air and hit me in the forehead. The speed and accuracy meant it could only have come from Nick, and I turned to stick my tongue out at him.

"Go sign us up!" he shouted, pointing to the line at the front of the class.

I raised my eyebrows and leaned closer, not sure if I'd heard correctly. "What?"

"Go sign Nick and me up!" said Parker. "We're in the middle of a paper football game."

I scowled, realizing what they meant. "Go sign your own team up!"

Nick and Parker exchanged a puzzled look, and Nick waved me over.

"What's with the attitude? You're the only person on the team who isn't busy so why can't you do it?"

"On the team?" I repeated. "Wait . . . you want us to compete together?" I couldn't help smiling.

144

"Well, yeah. It makes sense since all of our fates are inter-twined," said Parker.

"Very dramatic," said Nick.

I was thrilled and flattered that my brothers wanted me on their team, but I didn't dare give them the satisfaction of knowing it. "All right, all right." I rolled my eyes and went to get in line for the sign-up sheet.

"Hey, Alex!" Chloe hurried toward me with Trevor right behind. "You don't have to add our team. I already did. We're going to kick so much butt!"

"Oh!" I looked from her to Trevor. She'd actually sucked him in. "You guys are on the same team, huh?"

Trevor nodded but didn't look particularly thrilled.

"Well, I'm really sorry," I said, mainly to Trevor. "But my brothers asked me to join them, and I couldn't say no to my family."

Trevor frowned but nodded. "I under—"

"You what?!" squeaked Chloe.

Once again, I was blessed with getting to watch her undergo a nuclear meltdown.

"But you and I already agreed to be teammates! Forget your brothers! I want to win, Alex!"

"I know you do," I said. "But my brothers and I—"

"Can do something without one another for once," she snapped. "You owe me this, Alex!"

Trevor had wisely shifted several feet away to inspect a pencil sharpener.

"I don't owe you anything!" I said.

Chloe got within inches of my face. "In case you've already forgotten, *I* was the one who bragged about your leadership skills to Ms. Success!"

"Yeah, *after* you lied to her about what we'd been working on," I shot back. "Don't forget that I saved you."

Chloe's face turned bright red. "*And* I didn't tell anyone when you pushed me in the pool!"

I gritted my teeth. "I didn't push you, but I should have! You were acting crazy!"

"You were trying to steal—"

"I never tried to steal Trevor!" I shouted. "Emily did! And because she's not a raving lunatic, she actually got him!"

I paused for breath, and it was then that I realized the entire class was watching us. The three biggest sets of eyes in the room belonged to Ms. Success, Trevor, and Emily.

Nick cleared his throat and scooted past me. "Maybe *I* should just sign us up then."

Ms. Success pointed to Chloe and me, curling her finger inward. "Why don't we talk in my office?"

With one final glare at me, Chloe stormed out the door. After an apologetic smile to the class, I started to follow, but

Emily stopped me. Judging by the scowl on her face, this wouldn't be a go-get-'em-tiger talk.

"How could you?" she hissed, her voice shaking with anger. "I asked you to keep *one* secret. . . ."

I nodded vigorously. "I know, and I'm sorry. It just—"

She thrust a hand in my face to silence me. "You always have to have the last word, Alexis, but this time it's my turn. Friendship over."

Emily turned on her heel and walked away. And just like that I was back to being lonely Alex, the girl with no friends.

Except this time, it actually made me a little sad.

The bad thing about having a class with my brothers was that it gave them an extra chance to be nosy. After Ms. Success scolded us for our chump behavior and threatened to kick us out, I left the building to join Nick and Parker.

"You do know the goal is to *make* friends, right?" asked Parker.

Nick punched him. "I said 'be supportive,' not 'be yourself.'"

"And anyway, *I'm* not the problem," I said.

"I don't know," said Parker. "I'm pretty sure there were two girls back there trying to explode your head with their minds."

I let out an exasperated grunt. "Don't you have bigger things to worry about?"

"Like what?" Parker asked with a frown.

"Like *this*." I licked my hand and then rubbed it in his hair.

"Augh!" Parker sprinted off to check his reflection in a nearby car window. But unfortunately, that was only one brother down.

"What did you do to make Emily so mad?" asked Nick.

I threw my hands in the air. "Why does everyone assume it's *my* fault? Emily shouldn't be keeping her stupid relationship with Trevor a secret in the first place."

"Maybe not, but is that really your choice?" asked Nick.

"It was an accident," I said. "But Emily's such a drama queen that she doesn't see it that way. It's always about her and how things affect *her*." The more I talked about it, the more worked up I was getting. I didn't even see Chloe exit the building until she brushed past me.

I felt a momentary pang of guilt because she might have heard me mention Emily, but I quickly put it out of my mind and kept going. While we waited for Dad to show up, I rattled off a list of Emily's faults until Nick finally put a hand over my mouth.

"You were done venting a while ago," he said. "Now you're being mean."

I squirmed away. "I am not! I was just pointing out—"

"Good friends *don't*," he interrupted. "They make each other seem flawless."

"And the way you're describing Emily, she's a pitchfork short of being the devil," said Parker, rejoining us.

I frowned at him but didn't say anything. I hated to admit it, but both he and Nick were right. Instead of just being upset about this one event, I was adding it to a pile of Emily's other mistakes.

Nick noticed my silence and nudged me. "You and Emily *are* friends, right?"

"I don't know. Maybe?" I sighed. "If we *are* friends, I'm apparently not a very good one."

"That's all we've been trying to say," said Parker.

I punched him in the shoulder.

"This is new for Alex," said Nick, giving me a squeeze. "She's working on it."

I smiled gratefully at him and wondered if this was the time to mention Mom's note. But before I could, Dad pulled up to the curb.

"How was Champs?" he asked as we climbed in.

"Ms. Success is exploiting us for her film career," said Parker.

"I've made some new enemies," I added.

"And I accidentally swallowed the eraser off my pencil," said Nick.

Dad stared blankly at all of us. "But did the three of you *learn* anything?"

"I learned not to chew on my pencil," Nick said.

Dad sighed. "Well, that was money well spent."

"Speaking of money," said Parker, "we need to work on coming up with our three hundred-dollar championship entry fee."

Nick nodded. "My coach has some team laundry I could do that he'd pay me one hundred dollars for, so I'm all set with my share."

"I'm impressed," said Parker.

Nick waved him away. "It's just laundry."

"No, I'm impressed you could divide three hundred by three," said Parker with a wicked grin.

"Wait," said Dad. "So the three of you are on a team together?"

"Yep," I said.

"By choice?" asked Dad.

"Of course," said Nick with a laugh.

Dad beamed at all of us, and Parker groaned.

"Don't get weird and sentimental, Dad."

"I wouldn't dream of it," he said, forcing a serious face. "Carry on."

Parker gave a haughty sniff. "Well, *I've* thought of a few fund-raising ideas that harness the power of my intelligence."

"Meaning?" I asked.

"For a ten-dollar fee, people can give me their homework and I'll—"

"False," interrupted Dad. "You won't be doing anyone else's homework. In fact, I'm shocked you'd even consider it."

"Why are you shocked?" asked Parker. "We haven't learned about honesty in Champs yet."

We all laughed.

"What other ideas did you have, Parker?" asked Nick.

"None." Parker frowned. "All of mine involve slightly illegal efforts to aid my fellow man."

"Huh?" asked Nick.

"All his ideas involve cheating," I said. "I, on the other hand, have a perfectly legal idea. A hockey scrimmage, ten dollars per person to play. I talked to the manager of The Iceman, and he said I could rent one of the rinks for seventy-five dollars. If we can get two teams of twelve together, that's a one hundred and sixty-five dollar profit."

Parker rubbed his chin. "Not bad."

"Yeah, that's a clever idea," said Nick.

I smiled and patted myself on the back. "I agree. Well done, Alex!"

"What does the winner get?" asked Dad.

"Get?" I stopped my self-congratulation and frowned.

"I didn't think of that. I don't suppose they'd be happy just knowing they won?"

"Not unless you can buy pizza with happiness," said Nick.

"You could try getting some sponsors," said Dad. "You know, local businesses to donate something for being mentioned in your program."

"Dad, this is a scrimmage," I said. "There's not going to be a program. If anything, it'll be a torn-out piece of notebook paper with a grease stain on it."

"You could make a banner, though," said Nick. "And hang it on the boards."

"And mention the sponsors on flyers you use to advertise the scrimmage," said Parker.

"A banner?" I repeated. "I could actually put something I learned in hockey boosters to use."

Nick poked Parker. "So then it's up to you to come up with the rest of the money."

"Thirty-five dollars? No problem," said Parker.

"And since your portion is less, you have to help Alex find sponsors for her scrimmage," Nick continued.

Parker rolled his eyes. "Fine. We'll hit the pavement this weekend. But if my running blisters reopen, I won't be pleasant to live with."

I nodded. "Just like any other day."

Chapter 12 ✿

On Saturday, I was impressed to see Parker up and actually ready to go before noon. I was *not* impressed, however, to see him wearing our Champs shirt.

"Why are you dressed like that?" I asked as he left the bathroom.

"So businesses will find us more credible," he said. "They'll assume we're with an organization, and they'll be more likely to donate when they see our T-shirts."

"*Our* T-shirts?" I asked. "I think we can get the same message across if just one of us sports the star."

Parker crossed his arms. "But if I'm the only one in a Champs T-shirt, I'll look like an idiot."

"Yes," I said, "but maybe people will take pity on us and give money toward getting you a better wardrobe."

When he didn't budge, I sighed and went to change. After I re-emerged, I headed downstairs to find him eating breakfast and studying a map.

"What's that for?" I poured myself a bowl of cereal and joined him.

"I'm analyzing the businesses in the area near the rink," he said. "We should start with them, since their proximity makes them most likely to help."

"Uh-huh." I read over his shoulder. "And what could . . . Drapes 'n' More donate that a teenager would possibly want?"

He frowned at me. "Obviously we won't ask all the businesses."

"I don't know," I teased. "I think Toilet Town could make us a nice offer."

Parker dropped his map. "Well, what do *you* suggest?"

"The places close to the rink were a good idea," I admitted, "but the places popular with kids are better."

I pointed out a strip of restaurants and game and clothing shops a few blocks away. "Here. The Style Mile."

Parker sat quietly, chewing his lips while I chewed my cereal. "Fine," he said when I was almost done eating. "We'll try *your* way so I can prove you wrong."

After breakfast, we grabbed Dad from his office and ran into Nick in the hall.

"Where are you guys going?" he asked.

"The Style Mile," I said.

Nick's eyes lit up. "Ooh. I love that place. Give me a sec to get ready."

With a smirk, I turned to look at Parker, but he'd discovered an interesting piece of lint on his sleeve.

Dad dropped us off at the end of the mile and promised to pick us up later. "Good luck," he said. "Don't take any donations of livestock." Then he drove away.

"Where are you guys starting?" asked Nick.

"Aww. You want to help?" I asked.

"No, I want to make sure nobody sees us together." He nodded at our star shirts.

Parker and I frowned, and Nick pointed to the nearest game store. "I'll just hide in there."

We watched him go, and then Parker looked from me to the people walking past.

"Maybe the Champs T-shirts *were* a bad idea," he said. "Do you think someone would buy them from us?"

"Actually, I think they'd want *us* to pay *them*." I put an arm around his shoulder. "Come on. Let's try the pizza place first."

It was early enough that the parlor wasn't crowded yet,

so we had no problem talking to the owner. When she approached us, Parker smoothed out his T-shirt, fluffed his hair, and stepped forward to shake her hand.

"Madam," he said in his most professional voice. "As proprietor of this establishment, I conjecture that you're responsible for various marketing opportunities when they arise?"

The owner stared at Parker and scratched her head. "As the what?"

"What my brother's trying to say," I cut in, "is that we're collecting prizes for a hockey scrimmage, and we're wondering if you could donate anything."

The owner crossed her arms. "What's in it for me?"

"You'll be mentioned on the scrimmage flyers," I said. "And on a banner at the actual event."

She shook her head. "That's not enough."

Parker and I glanced at each other.

"Name your terms," said my brother.

"I'm short on help this week." The owner pointed to a swinging door behind her. "Dishes are stacking up in the kitchen and the floor's a mess. Clean it all up, and I'll donate two large pies."

Parker nodded. "It's a deal. Alex, get in there." He prodded me in the back, and I raised my eyebrows at him.

"Excuse me? I don't remember volunteering."

Parker smiled at the owner and pulled me aside. "You pick up dirty pennies in public places. Touching a few grungy plates and floors shouldn't be a problem."

"That's not the point," I said. "I'm not doing all the work while you sit around."

"I have to suffer too," he said. "As we speak, my hair is soaking up the scent of pizza."

The owner cleared her throat. "What's it gonna be, kids?"

I fixed Parker with a stern gaze. "You do the mopping and I'll do the dishes."

Five minutes later, I was up to my elbows in soapy foam and staring at a pile of plates and glasses.

"Be careful," said Parker. "If you break anything, you'll probably have to work here all night."

"Thanks for your concern." I scooped a pile of crusty silverware into the water. "Don't get your hair caught in the mop wringer."

In answer, Parker let the mop hit the floor with a wet splat. "This is actually pretty easy," he said. "I'm glad you took the harder task."

"Well, I didn't want your dainty lady fingers to turn into prunes," I said.

Parker didn't pick up on my sarcasm. "Where do you think we should go next? One of the shoe stores?"

"No. It'll mainly be guys at the scrimmage," I said. "And

I doubt they'd want twenty percent off wedge sandals."

After washing a stack of plates and pizza pans, I finally went back to the silverware I'd left soaking. One of the spoons I pulled out was bent in half. I showed my brother and he smirked.

"High-quality silverware *and* child labor in the kitchen," he said.

"Yes, but they're fancy enough to have flower vases!" I held one up.

"That's a drink carafe," said Parker. "It's just narrower on top so you can hold it when you pour water. Like a fancy pitcher."

"See? Fancy!" I set it down and went back to straightening the spoon, but it slipped out of my hand and flipped into the carafe.

"Ten points for Alex Evins!" I cheered.

"Quit playing and get back to work," said Parker. "My mop is starting to look nicer than my hair."

I reached into the carafe and grabbed the spoon, but when I tried to pull my hand out . . . it wouldn't budge.

"Uh-oh." I twisted my wrist and pulled, but there was no give. I jerked back, but my hand didn't move.

Trying not to panic, I turned to my brother. "Parker? I'm stuck."

He didn't look up from his mopping. "Yeah, this floor *is*

pretty gummy. I think they've been mopping it with soda."

I flung a fork at him. "No, I'm not stuck to the floor! I'm just stuck!"

He looked up and saw me waving a carafe-covered hand.

"Oh you've got to be kidding." He leaned the mop against the sink. "What happened?"

"I was trying to get the spoon out of the carafe."

He inspected the bottle. "Why didn't you tip it over and let the spoon fall out?"

I just stared at him. "Because I'm twelve, and I did not think of that."

"Okay, okay." He grabbed some liquid soap and squirted it on my hand. Then he tried twisting and pulling on the carafe. "Hmmm."

"Oh, wait! I'll just break myself free." I raised my hand to smash the bottle against the sink, but Parker stopped me. "Don't!"

I rolled my eyes. "There's a ton of these laying around. They're not going to miss one." I lifted my hand again, and Parker jumped between me and the sink.

"I'm not worried about the carafe, dummy. I'm worried about your hand!" he said. "If you break the glass, a piece of it could slice your skin open."

My eyes widened and I clutched the carafe to me protectively. "Oh."

"Just let me think." He paced in front of me and rubbed his chin. "When a rabbit gets caught in a snare, it usually escapes by chewing off its trapped leg."

I shook my head. "I'll learn to live with this bottle on my hand before that happens. And I will entertain myself by learning to twirl the spoon."

Parker stopped and smacked himself in the forehead. "You're still holding the spoon! Let it go. Your fist is causing your hand to take up more space."

I released the spoon and jerked on the carafe. "It's not working!"

Parker grabbed my shoulders. "Stop panicking. You're only causing your hand to swell. Just relax and breathe." He walked away.

"Don't go!" I said, sliding across the wet floor after him.

Parker gave me a weird look. "You're my sister. I'm not leaving you." He reached into the ice maker and scooped up a handful of cubes. "Chill out." He grinned at his own stupid pun.

"Ha ha," I said.

He held the freezing water against my wrist, and gently twisted the carafe again.

I gasped as my hand inched free. "It's working!"

"Of course it's working," said Parker, setting the carafe on the counter. "I'm a genius."

I smiled at him and stole a hug. "Thanks, Parker."

He hugged me back. "Let's finish up and get the heck out of here."

"Agreed." I went back to tackling dishes and Parker finished the floors. When he was done, he shifted over to help me, and after an hour or so, we finally stepped away from the sink.

"Those better be some *large* pizzas," I said.

"No doubt." Parker pushed the mop bucket out the back door. "Could you help me dump this water? I think the floor filth added an extra ten pounds, and I'd really prefer *not* to get it all over my shoes."

I followed him to the rear patio, which consisted of nothing but a dumpster on one side and a flower bed on the other, surrounded by towering brick walls.

"Once again, fancy," I said, shutting the door behind me.

"At least nobody's getting in to steal the garbage." Parker nodded to the walls. "Or getting out. So you'd better make sure—" He turned and froze, staring at something behind me.

"What?" I got a sinking feeling in my stomach. "The back door locks automatically, doesn't it?" I rushed over and jiggled the knob, but the door wouldn't budge. "Um." I faced Parker and said in small voice, "We may both be stuck this time."

To his credit, Parker didn't get mad or try to use me as a battering ram to knock the door down. "If we have to make the owner come rescue us, that's not gonna look good." He glanced around the back patio. "That dumpster should be tall enough."

"For what?" I asked.

"For me to reach the top of the wall."

I wrinkled my forehead. "Parker, that's going to take a lot of upper-body strength, and you've only got . . . well, none."

"You think so?" he asked.

The next thing I knew, he was running full speed toward the brick wall beside the dumpster. His right foot left the ground, and he used it to kick off the wall and launch himself on top of the trash container.

"Woah." I said, blinking hard. "Where did you learn to move like that?"

"Trust me, you get threatened by enough bullies, you can climb a spiderweb if you have to," he said. "Want to give it a try?"

I glanced from my feet to the wall to the dumpster. "Can I just climb partway and you pull me up?"

He looked doubtful. "Sure, but your Champs shirt will be ruined."

"Sold!" I scrambled up the front of the dumpster, and Parker dragged me to the top.

From there we both peered over the other side of the brick wall to the ground far, far below.

"You go first," I told him. "That way I'll have something soft to land on."

He smirked at me. "Or we could just use the ladder."

"Where?" I glanced around. Several feet to my left, a metal ladder was bolted into the side of the building. "That'll work."

But getting to the ladder required crawling along the top of the brick wall.

"I'll go first," said Parker. "That way you can watch—"

"Uh, no. You can watch me," I said, climbing onto the wall.

"Careful," said Parker, holding his hands in the air as if to steady me.

"I'm fine," I said, zipping along the wall. Balance had never been a problem for me, and I'd spent plenty of my pranking days walking around on rooftops. I could have shown off and actually gotten to my feet, but Parker already looked like he might pass out.

When I reached the ladder, Parker exhaled an audible sigh of relief. "You've got good balance."

"It's all in the knees," I said.

He was almost as quick as I'd been, and when we were both back on the ground, we couldn't help grinning.

"That was kind of fun," I said.

"That was kind of stupid," said an angry Evins voice that did *not* belong to Parker.

Nick was walking toward us from the front of the alley, arms crossed with his eyebrows set in a furious V. "*What* were you doing up there?" He grabbed my wrist where it was red from my efforts to remove the carafe. "And what happened to your arm?"

"I got it stuck in something when I was trying to wash dishes," I said.

Without a word, he tugged me into the pizza parlor and demanded to talk to the owner.

"Are you done with the dishes?" she asked when she saw me.

"Oh, she's done all right," Nick snapped at the woman. "Why was my twelve-year-old sister on top of a twenty-foot wall with nothing under her but the pavement?"

His voice was getting louder, and people were starting to stare.

The owner shook her head. "I didn't send her outside. I had her washing dishes."

"And she hurt herself doing *that*." He pointed to the red marks on my arm. "All she wanted was a donation for her club scrimmage. What kind of person are you?"

The owner glanced around the restaurant, her face turning a brilliant pink.

"I . . . I didn't mean." She held her arms open. "She can have the free pizzas now."

"You mean the ones she already earned?" spoke up Parker.

Knowing that all her patrons were watching her, the woman forced a smile. "How about a pizza party for whoever wins the scrimmage?"

Several people clapped, and Nick's expression finally relaxed. "That's fair. Thank you."

While we waited for the owner to write up a voucher, a man came over to talk to us.

"What club are you a part of?" he asked, giving the Champs star a scrutinizing gaze.

Nick explained about Champs and the championship, and the man rubbed his jaw.

"I like your enthusiasm. How about I contribute a prize for your scrimmage?" he asked. "I own the music store a few buildings over, and I could give fifteen dollar gift certificates to the winning team."

My jaw dropped. With a pizza party *and* gift certificates, we'd fill every spot on the two teams. I was too stunned to say anything, so Parker filled the void.

"Thank you so much! That'd be great! Your contribution is well-appreciated. Without the support of—"

"No problem," said the man, fending off Parker's thanks. "You look like a sweet family."

The Evil Evinses looked at one another and laughed.

Chapter 13 ❀

Things seemed to be going so well between my brothers and I that I knew *now* was the time to bring up Mom's note. And since I'd ended a meal the last time I'd mentioned her, I decided it was best to get it over with *before* lunch.

"Can I talk to you guys about something serious?" I asked as we walked to the restaurant.

"Not if it's something seriously girlie," said Parker.

Nick elbowed him. "What is it, Alex?"

"It's about Mom."

Neither one of them responded, and since it wasn't an outright no, I continued. "It's about Mom meeting with you guys."

Both of my brothers slowed their pace and exchanged a glance. I waved a hand between them.

"No twin telepathy," I said.

Parker cleared his throat. "What meeting are you talking about, Alex? We never met with her."

I rolled my eyes. "First of all, you're a terrible liar. Second of all, I found this note from Mom."

I fished it out of my pocket and did my best to smooth it flat. The paper was getting wrinkled and worn from all the time it spent traveling between various pairs of jeans.

Nick took the note and read it, eyes widening.

"You've never seen that before, have you?" I asked.

The slightest flicker of emotion crossed Nick's face, but he set his jaw and said, "Nope."

Then he crumpled the note and threw it in the street.

"Hey!" I pushed him out of the way and rescued my wadded-up Mom memento. "Why'd you do that?"

"What did it say?" Parker asked him.

"More of her lies," said Nick. "How she was sorry about the meeting and how she loved us."

Parker snorted. "That doesn't belong in the street."

"*Thank* you," I said.

"It belongs in the garbage." Parker tried to snatch it from me, but I was too quick.

"Stop it!" I tucked the note back into the safety of my pocket. "Tell me what happened with Mom."

Nick shook his head. "Just let it go."

"No! Don't shut me out like Dad does. She said she loved me, so why didn't she—?"

Nick rounded on me, his shoulders tense and his nostrils flaring. "I *said*, let it go!" he yelled.

I stumbled away from him in surprise. People on the sidewalk were staring at us now, so Parker pushed Nick and me into an alleyway. For once, my troublemaking brother played the role of peacemaker.

"Nick, just calm down," said Parker. "Alex, it's not that she didn't want to see you. It's that *we* didn't want you to see *her*."

I let out a cry of disgust. "You didn't want to share her?! You selfish—"

"We were trying to protect you," cut in Nick, his face returning to its normal color. "We were afraid she was going to hurt the family again." He rubbed his neck in irritation. "And we were right."

My forehead wrinkled. "I don't understand."

Parker took a deep breath before speaking. "I wasn't lying when I said we never met with Mom. We were supposed to, but she never showed up."

Instantly, I felt ashamed of my accusations.

"Oh," I said.

"We never mentioned it because we didn't want to make you feel bad," said Nick. "Plus, Dad was *really* angry."

"Which is why he told her to quit sending gifts," I mumbled.

"Pretty much," said Nick.

The three of us stood in silence for a moment, alternately looking at one another or the ground. My poor, sweet brothers had secretly lived through this huge hurt and disappointment, doing everything they could to protect me from it.

Emotions started to overwhelm me, but I couldn't let them see that I was upset. They'd worked too hard to make sure something like this wouldn't happen. I cleared the lump from my throat and blinked my eyes dry. When I could trust myself to speak, I said, "I'm sorry. I never should have brought it up."

Nick shook his head. "You needed to find out. We just hoped it would be later, like when you were eighty." He smiled weakly and put an arm around my shoulder. "I'm sorry for yelling."

I leaned against him. "It's all right. I kind of deserved it."

"Hey!" Parker forced his way between us. "How come you let Nick get away with yelling and not me?"

I put my arms around both my brothers. "Because Nick yells about once a year. You have it on your daily to–do list."

Parker scoffed. "Doubtful!"

"You yelled at a ladybug this morning," said Nick, steering us out of the alley.

"*That* was because I stepped on it with bare feet."

"I also heard you yelling in the shower," I said.

"*That* was because someone wrote 'diva detangler' on my conditioner."

Nick and I exchanged a high-five.

"Enjoy that," said Parker. "Because neither of you can imagine the revenge I have in store."

I squinted thoughtfully. "Does it involve some sort of . . . yelling?"

Nick laughed, and even Parker smiled.

I could joke about revenge with Parker, but on Monday morning I was definitely worried about what Emily and Chloe might do. While I canvassed the building with flyers for the scrimmage, I had to simultaneously avoid their nefarious clutches. It wasn't that I was unwilling to apologize to Emily or that I was afraid of Chloe, but knowing my luck, they'd joined forces to create a super-terror.

Still, I knew I'd have to face both girls in PE, especially since we'd moved on to the presidential fitness challenge. That involved a *lot* more standing around, waiting to be tested . . . and a lot more time for the girls to plot a revenge much harsher than Parker's yelling.

Monday we were doing the rope climb, and since fate was feeling hilariously cruel, I was chosen to climb against Chloe.

While we waited in line, however, she just nodded. "Hey, Alex."

"Heeey?" I let my greeting end as a question.

"Problem?" she asked, smiling innocently.

I blinked at her. "You don't remember last Thursday? When we got in that big fight?"

Chloe waved a dismissive hand. "Oh, I'm over that."

"Really?" I asked.

"Yep. I don't have time for negative energy in my life. That includes backstabbers like you." She smiled like she hadn't just insulted me.

"Uh, just because I'm not on your team doesn't mean I'm stabbing you in the back," I said.

"Actually, I was talking about my feelings for Trevor," she said, tilting her head to the side. "You know . . . how I told you I liked him and then you betrayed me by hooking him up with Emily?"

"What? I would *never*!" I argued.

The girls in front of us turned around, and I smiled, pointing at Chloe. "She was asking if I liked Lindsay Lohan."

Chloe waited for them to turn away before she said,

"Emily couldn't have possibly gotten him herself. The girl's a nightmare. Monsters are afraid of finding *her* under the bed."

I shook my head. "She's got it way more together than you do."

Chloe lifted a hand to block me out. "Whatever. Just know that your little plan backfired. Since everyone has full teams, Trevor doesn't have a choice *but* to work with me. He and I are going to win and he'll see that *I'm* the right girl for him." She said the last words a little louder and smirked in Emily's direction. "So I'm not upset. I just feel pity for you." She tilted her head to one side and pouted her bottom lip.

I rolled my eyes as we stepped up to the ropes. "*You* pity *me?*"

She nodded. "You and your brothers don't stand a chance. The scrawny one, what's his name, Parker? He'll be out after the first obstacle. And the cute but clueless one . . . Nick, right? He'll probably spend most of his time figuring out his shoelaces."

If the teacher hadn't been standing right there, I would have strangled Chloe with my climbing rope.

"My brothers and I will do just fine," I said, fixing her with a steely gaze.

The teacher blew the whistle, and it was almost as if someone had put a springboard beneath Chloe and me. We both leapt up the rope and hurried our climb, rapidly bringing fist over fist. The inside of my legs burned from the coarseness of the rope, but I didn't slow my pace.

Unfortunately, Chloe still managed to inch ahead of me and ring the bell at the top about ten seconds before I could.

Holding on with just one hand and coiling a leg around the rope, she smirked at me. "Like I said, you don't stand a chance." Then she loosened her grip just enough so that the rope whizzed through her fingers as she rapidly descended to the floor.

"Please." I positioned myself like she had and relaxed my grip. As soon as I started to drop, I felt the burn from the rope even worse than before, like I was sliding down a razor blade and peeling off my skin.

When I reached the ground, I pressed my lips together and fought back a cry of pain. I didn't dare glance at my hand or thighs, but I had a feeling they were probably the color and texture of tomato paste. The rest of the class was watching me and some were wincing in sympathy pain. Chloe alone was smiling.

"May the best girl win," I grunted at her. Then I sauntered off as casually as I could.

Of course, Emily chose the one moment that I couldn't run away to engage me in conversation.

"Are you okay?" she asked, following me to the locker room.

"I'm fine," I said, forcing a smile.

"You're walking like you just climbed off a really fat horse."

I paused and faced her. "Emily, in ten seconds I'm going to black out from a severe rope burn. If you came to yell at me about Trevor some more, you might want to make it quick."

"Uh, no." Emily stared down at her hands. "Actually, I wanted to thank you for sticking up for me and to say I'm sorry."

I collapsed on a bench from both surprise and pain. "What?"

She shrugged sheepishly. "I shouldn't have yelled at you and made you keep Trevor a secret. You've always been super nice where he's involved."

Being the perfectionist that she was, I knew it took a lot for Emily to admit she'd done something wrong.

"It's okay," I said with an encouraging smile. "But thanks."

"Sure." Emily started twisting her hands back and forth.

"Was there something else?" I asked.

"Don't be mad," she said.

"Uh-oh."

"But ever since you showed me that note from your mom, I've been thinking," said Emily. "It stinks that you never got closure with her."

My forehead wrinkled in confusion. "Okaaay."

She took a deep breath. "Well, my stepmom has connections *everywhere*, and she was able to get a phone number for *your* mom."

My heart dropped into the pit of my stomach. "What?"

"It's her voice mail at the research base here in the States." Emily lowered her eyes and handed me a piece of paper. "You don't have to call, but I wanted you to have the option."

I stared at the number, thinking of the photo albums, Mom's note, and my brothers. I reached out a hand to Emily.

"Let me borrow your cell phone."

Her face lit up. "Really? You're going to call her now?" Emily opened her locker and dug through her purse.

"Now's as good a time as any," I said, taking a deep breath as she handed me the phone. My fingers trembled a little when I dialed, but as soon as the voice mail picked up, all my fear vanished.

And it was replaced with anger.

"Hey, *Mom*," I said in my most sarcastic voice. "It's your daughter. You know, the one you abandoned?"

The smile on Emily's face dropped in horror.

"I just wanted you to know that Nick, Parker, Dad, and I are all doing fine," I said.

Emily tried to grab her phone but I twisted out of reach.

"In fact, we're doing *so* fine that we don't need your stupid birthday money, we don't need your stupid Christmas money, and we don't need *you*."

I snapped the phone shut and shoved it in Emily's hands. She stared at it for a moment before silently putting it in her pocket.

But that wasn't the reaction I wanted.

I wanted Emily to yell at me for being so rude after she went to all that trouble and for ruining my one chance to connect with my mother. I wanted her to storm off because I'd failed so miserably at bringing my family back together.

Instead, Emily simply gave me a sad smile. "What *happened*, Alexis?"

I dropped to the floor and hugged my knees to my chest. Then I cried. Emily sat beside me and listened as I told her everything. Soon she was crying too, and we put our arms around each other.

We sat like that for several minutes until I started having trouble breathing. Finally, I raised my head and wiped my eyes.

"Are you mad at me?" asked Emily.

I shook my head.

"Good," she said. "Because I wouldn't have forced that phone number on you if I'd known."

Despite my tears, I smiled. "Yes, you would have."

She smiled back. "Okay, you're right. But I would have taken you to an amusement park first to put you in a better mood."

I actually laughed out loud. As strange as it seemed, I felt comforted by Emily's presence for once, not weirded out. It was nice to have someone outside the family to share my darkest secrets with, someone who could feel with me and not be embarrassed. It was nice to have someone watching out for me, not because they had to, but because they wanted to.

It was nice to have a true friend.

Girls were filing in from the gym, stopping to check on me, but thankfully I could blame my tears on the rope burns.

I spent the entire walk home that afternoon debating whether or not I should share what I'd done with my brothers. Would they be happy I told her off? Or angry that I didn't talk to them first?

My thoughts were put on hold when I spotted a strange truck in our driveway, carrying at least twenty large canvas bags. I quickened my pace to get a closer look as a man emerged from the house, followed by Nick and Parker. The man waved when he saw me, and I realized it was Nick's football coach.

I waved back and watched as Nick and Parker helped the man pull the bags off the truck and toss them onto the driveway. The drawstring on one of the bags was loose, and when it shifted open, I saw a rubberized name and number written on a jersey.

Then I remembered what Nick had told us several days before: "My coach has some team laundry I could do. . . ."

I sighed and rolled up my sleeves. If Nick could help me get a pizza party for *my* portion of the fund-raiser, I could at least scrub a jersey or two.

But smelly guy socks were out of the question.

❋ Chapter 14

Never underestimate the power of persuasion," Ms. Success told us Thursday night. "Girls," she said as she pointed around the room, "with this skill, you can get a boy to pay your way at the movies. Boys, with this skill, you can get free M&M's at the concession stand."

Trevor frowned at me. "Sounds better to be the girl."

"I think Emily has a wig you can borrow," I whispered back.

"We already know a person's name is the most important thing about them." Ms. Success jerked her head toward Parker, daring him to correct her. "But this can also be said of their emotions. Appeal to someone's feelings, and you can easily win them over."

She pointed to a sentence she'd written on the board, and we all chanted, "Open hearts lead to open wallets."

For the next half hour, Ms. Success lectured on persuasive techniques, and when she was finished, Emily walked around the room and handed each of us blue drawstring pouches.

"You should each be receiving twenty pieces of Champs change." Ms. Success raised her voice to be heard among the clinking of coins. "Your task for the remainder of class is to collect the most Champs change from your classmates, using the power of persuasion."

I opened my pouch and poured out a handful of gold coins with a star on one side and Ms. Success's grinning face on the other.

"Huh," I said. "That's odd."

Trevor snorted. "You think it's odd that Ms. Success would put herself on money?"

"No, I think it's odd that she couldn't get the government to put her on *actual* money," I said with a smirk.

"Don't think I didn't try," said Ms. Success from directly behind me.

I cringed and twisted around, smiling up at her apologetically. Ms. Success ignored me and addressed the class.

"Don't take this lightly, folks. Because whoever collects the most money wins *this*." She held out a rolled-up piece of paper tied with ribbon.

People shifted forward in their seats, trying to see what was inside.

"This beauty," she said with a smile, "contains a list of the obstacles in the Champs Championship."

Instantly, the volume in the classroom increased, and even I couldn't help getting a little excited. Up until now, nobody had had a chance of knowing the challenges since Ms. Success changed them every year.

As soon as she gave the okay, people jumped out of their seats and started bargaining with one another for Champs change. I started to get up too, but when I pushed away from the table I saw that Trevor had a gigantic gash across one knee.

"Ouch. *What* happened?" I asked.

"Well, it turns out I can only jump *four* cars with my bike," he said, rubbing the wound.

My eyes widened. "Really?"

"Nah." He grinned. "Chloe and I started training last weekend for the championship."

I dropped back onto my seat. "You've been training? How? We don't even know what the obstacles are."

"Not specifically," said Trevor. He raised an eyebrow. "But if you give me all of your fake money, I'll let you in on a secret."

I sized him up for a moment before handing over my bag of Champs change. "Deal."

He looked around and leaned toward me. "It's supposed to be modeled after the Sandhurst Military Skills competition at West Point," he whispered.

"Sandhurst?" I repeated, opening my notebook. "How do you spell it?"

Trevor held up a colored sheet of paper and studied it. "Let's see. S-a-n-d . . ."

I stopped writing when I saw the paper, and Trevor grinned. "Ms. Success had a stack of these on her desk."

I snatched the page from him and read:

> Parents, a reminder that this Sunday is
> the Champs Championship and a wonderful
> opportunity to see your child shine! Our
> obstacle course will prove to be a challenge,
> as it is modeled after West Point's own
> Sandhurst . . .

"Hey!" I lowered the paper. "You tricked me!"

I reached for my Champs change, but Trevor was already pouring the coins into his own bag. "Thanks for the contribution. Now I can buy some M&M's at the concession stand."

I sighed and pulled back my hand. "You earned it, I suppose. But have you really been training?"

"Yep," he said. "I mean, we didn't know about Sandhurst until now, but most obstacle courses are the same."

I frowned. "When are you going to have time for fund-raising?"

"Already done," he said, rubbing his palms together. "Chloe's been saving her babysitting money so all I had to do was mow a few lawns to keep from feeling guilty, and we jumped right into training."

"Oh. Well, good for you." I slumped on my stool, feeling more than a little discouraged. I'd been so proud of my hockey scrimmage, the prizes we'd earned, and the money we'd gotten from laundry, but apparently we were still behind. Chloe was already winning.

Trevor must have noticed that I was feeling dejected because he bumped my shoulder with his own. "Cheer up. We still haven't gotten the fire-making down."

If it was possible, I slouched even lower. To my complete and utter dismay, Chloe chose that moment to saunter over, shaking a bulging bag of Champs change.

"I think I'll come sit with the best and brightest." She

smiled at Trevor, then glanced my way. "Oh. And Alex."

I kept quiet even though her snub wasn't wasted on me. It was, however, wasted on Trevor.

"Hey, Chloe!" he said. "Wow, that's a lot of money."

She smiled and dropped the bag on the table with a *thunk*. "I've got social skills, something a few people in this class lack." Her eyes flitted to me. "All I have to do is say hello, and people practically throw money at me."

"Oh, like a street performer?" I couldn't help asking. "What's your talent? Playing a fiddle with your feet?"

Chloe's smile wavered a little, but she simply turned her back to me. "Do you still have your Champs change?" she asked Trevor.

"And Alex's." He grinned apologetically at me and handed his bag to Chloe.

"Then I'm going to go collect *our* list of obstacles." She squeezed his arm and winked at me. "And my talent is winning. You should try it some time."

When Dad pulled up to the curb after class, I leapt into the front seat before the car was even in park.

"We need flint," I told him. "And lots of wood."

He glanced past me to my brothers. "Should I be concerned?"

"It's for Champs," I said. "Nick, Parker, and I need to practice making fires."

"Isn't that what got you into trouble in the first place?" asked Dad.

"Yeah, but I don't think they're going to let me bring a Flaming #2 to the contest," I said. "We need to start a fire from scratch."

"I can do that," said Nick.

I frowned at him. "*Without* putting wet socks in the microwave."

"Oh." Nick shook his head. "Then never mind."

"Practicing wouldn't be a bad idea," said Parker. "We can at least be prepared for one of the challenges."

"All right," said Dad, putting the car in gear. "What do you plan to use for tinder?"

My brothers and I looked at one another.

"Huh?"

"What are you going to use to hold the spark until the wood catches on fire?" asked Dad.

"I've got just the thing." Parker held up his copy of *The Secrets of Success*, and Nick and I laughed. "She did say it would come in handy outside of class."

"Clever . . . but no," said Dad, smirking. "You won't have access to paper at the competition."

"There'll be leaves and pine needles on the ground," said Parker. "We'll use the paper for practice."

"All right, but let's also make sure we stay out of Mr.

186

McGuire's sight," Dad said. "The last thing we need is for him to think I'm teaching you how to commit arson."

I turned to face Dad. "You're going to help us?"

He shrugged. "I'm not a wilderness expert, but I've had to start a few fires from scratch so I can give you some pointers. Unless you want to do it on your own."

"No, we'd like you to be there," said Parker with a smile.

For the next few hours, Dad showed us how to strike the flint and get a good flame going. Nick was excellent at getting the sparks to fly, and Parker, being *so* full of hot air, could blow on the embers to create flames. I, of course, proved to be the most valuable, stacking the wood so it would burn just right and providing the marshmallows for toasting.

When Dad finally decided to retreat to his office, I searched the internet for the Sandhurst competition and showed it to my brothers.

"That doesn't look too bad," said Nick.

"Yeah, if we're with *those* guys," Parker nodded at the army platoon running the course. "Somehow I don't see us climbing a vertical wall in ten seconds."

"All we really have to do is complete the obstacles and start the fire," said Nick. "We're not required to take first place."

Parker and I stared aghast at him until he nodded.

"Yeah, okay. I want to win too."

"Trevor and Chloe have been training," I said. "Maybe we could try that."

"When?" asked Nick. "I've got football tomorrow night, and Saturday we'll be busy with the hockey scrimmage. Then the championship's on Sunday."

I bit my lip. We'd be going into the contest blind, with Nick as our only muscle, unless Parker had something hidden up his sleeve . . . or in his hair.

"We'll get through it," said Nick, noticing the worried look on my face.

"I know," I said. "I just don't want you to have to carry me and Parker."

"I don't mind if you carry me," Parker told him. "It'll be good servant training for you."

Nick gave him a wry smile. "Since we can't actually practice on a real course, why don't we at least talk about how we'd deal with these obstacles?"

And up until bedtime, that's what we did.

My biggest fear was that Nick would injure himself in his football game, but thankfully, he made it through safe and sound. On Saturday morning, he, Parker, and I got to The Iceman early so we could set up for the scrimmage. Or rather, so Nick and I could set up while Parker complained about how the cold was affecting his "athlete's legs."

"You don't have 'athlete's legs,'" I told him, filling a water cooler and hefting it onto a table. "You barely have chicken's legs."

"For your information, the chicken is related to the Tyrannosaurus rex," said Parker.

"Which had no upper body strength," I said, giving him a quick once-over. "What a strange coincidence."

Nick appeared and handed me a set of keys.

"What are these for?" I asked.

"The rink gates." He pointed to the huge iron gates that wrapped around each rink like a cage. "Hang on tight to them. I'm going to see who's playing today."

While we waited, I figured I might as well open one of the rinks, so I walked over to a padlock and searched for the matching key.

"Here, let me help." Parker snatched the keys away. "You'll put the wrong one in and get it stuck."

"No, I won't!" I jerked the key ring out of his hands, but my fingers were still slippery and wet from filling the water cooler. The keys flew into the air . . . and through the bars of the locked gate.

For a moment, Parker and I just stood there, watching as the keys hit the ice with a metallic *clink*. Then the horrible reality of the situation struck me.

We'd lost our one way of getting into the rink.

"No!" I cried, lunging forward and reaching through the bars. The keys were still several yards out of my reach.

I wheeled on Parker. "Look what you did!"

"Me?!" He crossed his arms. "I've got the legs of a chicken and the upper body of a T. rex. I hardly think I'm capable."

"Ohhh, this can't be happening!" I put my arm through the gate again and waved it back and forth, grabbing nothing but air.

"If you're trying to fly, I'd give it a go with both arms," said Parker.

"Shut up!" I grabbed a spare hockey stick off the rack and slid it between the grates, thrusting it at the keys, which promptly slid farther away. I pointed at Parker. "Don't . . . say . . . a . . . word."

"What's going on?" asked Nick.

He came toward us, followed by a sizable crowd of players wielding hockey sticks. Parker stepped into their line of sight so the keys weren't visible, and I grabbed Nick's arm and pulled him away.

"We can't get into the rink!" I whispered.

"What? I just gave you the keys!" he said.

I pointed onto the ice and Nick sighed.

"So the phrase 'hang on tight' means nothing to you?"

I wrung my hands together and glanced past him to the crowd. "What are we going to do?"

"Let me think," he said, rubbing his chin.

Parker laughed, but when Nick frowned at him, he stopped.

"Sorry. I thought you were joking."

Nick glanced at the hockey equipment and then at the players. "Alex, get everyone's chewing gum."

I tilted my head to one side. "Excuse me?"

"Almost all of these guys are chewing gum. Get them to spit it into your palm."

"Ugh!" I tucked both hands under my armpits. "Let's just buy ice from the market and put it in a kiddie pool. They can play on that."

"Alex . . . the gum," said Nick with a no-nonsense frown.

"Fine," I groaned.

"Parker, help me get some skate laces."

"Uh, okay." Parker's confused look carried over to the players as I made them spit their gum into my hand while Nick asked a few to unlace their skates.

When he had enough laces, he tied them end-to-end and then to the grill of a hockey mask. After that, he placed gum all around the back edges of the mask and tested the weight in his hand. Stepping up to the gate around the rink, he flung the mask through the bars and past the keys.

The mask landed on the ice, but because it fell gum-side down, it didn't skid out of control. Pulling on the skate laces, Nick dragged the mask back toward him. The front of it caught the keys and Nick was able to reel them in.

I gaped in amazement as he jingled the keys in front of me. "Ta-da!"

"That . . . that was awesome!" I said. "How did you even think to put that stuff together?"

He shrugged and unlocked the gate. "Just resourceful, I guess."

We returned everyone's skate laces (nobody wanted their gum back), and the players took to the ice to practice. My brothers and I sat in the bleachers, and a crowd filled in around us. I started to feel a warmth growing inside me, but it wasn't because of the mass of bodies. I was slowly realizing just how amazing my brothers were . . . and that we might actually have a fighting chance against Chloe and her crew.

Chapter 15 ✿

Sunday morning, my brothers and I received the air horn alarm clock experience again, but since Dad started at the other end of the hall, I simply pulled the covers over my head and rolled over.

"Wake up, Champ!" crowed a female voice.

Clearly *not* my dad.

I flipped over to see a gigantic star standing beside my bed.

"Augh!" I screamed and scooted against the wall.

"Alexis!" boomed Ms. Success. Her face, painted yellow, peeked out from the center of the star. "So nice of you to join the world of the living." She waddled to my window and drew back the curtains.

I sat up and rubbed my eyes. "What . . . what are you doing here besides bringing my worst nightmare to life?"

Emily at least had the common courtesy to stick to the hedges outside. Maybe this was part of the Champs course, hand-to-hand combat in my pajamas with the teacher. Or maybe all this time she'd secretly been dating . . .

"Dad!" I screamed.

Ms. Success winced and wiggled a star-point finger in her ear. "Wonderful set of lungs, Alexis. Save 'em for the course."

Footsteps thundered down the hall, and Nick and Parker ran into my room.

"Alex, what's . . . woah!" Nick stopped short at seeing Ms. Success. "Hey, uh, Coach."

"This used to be such a *normal* place." Parker brought his hands to his head.

Ms. Success clucked her tongue. "Traditionally I get a better response when I visit students."

"So this isn't your first home invasion?" I asked, drawing my blankets up.

Dad appeared behind Nick and Parker, smiling. "Oh, good. I see you got your wake-up call."

Parker turned to face him. "*You* let her in?"

"What else did you expect?" asked Ms. Success. "That I'd rappel off the roof and come crashing through a window like SWAT?"

"Okay, but *why* are you here?" I asked.

"It's a tradition for me to visit students on championship day, make sure they're fit for competition, and wish them good luck," she said, giving me a star's version of a thumbs-up. "So good luck!" She swiveled to show the thumb to my brothers.

"Uh, thanks." Nick mirrored her gesture and elbowed Parker to do the same.

"Alex?" Dad prompted from behind them.

I forced my thumb into the air. "You couldn't have sent a fruit basket instead?"

"Who says I didn't?" She winked at me and headed for the door. "It was nice to see you kids. I'm glad you sleep in pajamas." She winced. "I wasn't so lucky at the last house."

Nick and Parker stepped aside so she could pass through, and Dad walked Ms. Success downstairs.

"Amazing," said Parker, shaking his head. "This goes right behind 'covered in bees' as the worst way to wake up."

We dressed in our Champs T-shirts and athletic shorts, and went downstairs for breakfast. Sure enough, there was a fruit basket sitting in the center of the kitchen table.

"Well, *that* at least was nice of her," said Nick. He pulled a banana out of the basket, along with a small white card. "'To Sharon,' he read, 'I had fun on our date. Paul.'"

Nick lifted his head. "She gave us used fruit."

"And coffee filters, for some reason," said Dad, holding them up.

My brothers and I grinned at each other.

"Well, my thanks to Paul," said Parker, grabbing an apple and biting into it. "Although we need some *real* fuel for today."

"I'm one step ahead of you," said Dad, balancing three plates on his arm. They were laden with eggs, fried potatoes, bacon, and toast.

"Wow," said Nick. "So what are Alex and Parker going to eat?"

The three of us sat and tucked into our meals while Dad brought over orange juice and chocolate milk. He took his chair at the head of the table and smiled as he watched us.

Parker stopped mid-chew. "I feel like it's feeding time at the zoo."

Dad leaned forward and clasped his hands in front of him. "I just wanted to say that I'm very proud of the three of you. You've come further than I thought possible, individually and as a team."

"As a family," I corrected him.

Dad smiled and kissed my forehead. "You're right."

I smirked at my brothers. "Put that one in the record books."

"We're proud of you too, Dad," said Parker, turning a little red.

Dad cocked his head. "Why's that?"

"Well . . . because since we started Champs, you've been there for us a lot more than you used to be."

Dad's face fell.

"I mean you're always there," Parker corrected quickly. "And we appreciate it."

"Yeah. Except now we get bonus time," said Nick.

Dad shook his head. "You're right. And you were right when you first said it a few weeks ago. I'm not there enough."

"You do great," I said. "Considering you've had to raise us on your own."

"Yeah, we're not on drugs or covered in tattoos," said Parker. "And Alex only has one felony under her belt so far."

"Lighting the neighbor's couch on fire wasn't a felony," I pointed out. "The courts would call it criminal mischief."

Dad raised an eyebrow. "How disturbing that you know that."

"The point," said Nick, "is that you're a way better parent than certain others, who shall remain nameless, ever were."

Guilt tugged at the corner of my mind, remembering my voice mail to Mom, but I simply nodded in agreement.

"Thank you for that sentiment." Dad scraped his chair back. "And now, I've got presents for the three of you."

He disappeared into his office and returned with a small plastic bag. "Sorry I didn't wrap them," he said, plunking the bag between us on the table.

Parker grabbed it and pulled out a shiny, red Swiss Army knife.

"Cool," said Nick, reaching into the bag and pulling out the same.

"It's the Ranger version," said Dad. "I checked with Ms. Success, and it's completely legal to use in the competition."

Nick pulled at the bits of metal tucked away. "We've got scissors, a saw. . . . Oh yeah, this'll definitely come in handy." He passed the bag to me. "Thanks, Dad."

Dad nodded. "I just want you all to do your best."

"We will," I said, giving him a hug.

"And I'll still be proud of you no matter what place you get," he said. "As long as it's not last."

We laughed and finished breakfast, then left the house a little late after Parker (and his hair) realized people might be taking pictures. Since we were the last team to arrive at the championship, that was where Ms. Success placed us for competing order. Unfortunately, we still couldn't see the obstacle course since it was surrounded by a forest of pine trees.

Emily was there, too, standing by herself with a murderous look in her eyes. I walked over to greet her, but she stopped me when I was still a few feet away.

"As championship co-coordinator, I'm not allowed to talk to any of the competitors," she said, frowning. "Even if it's to tell them to stop drooling all over my crush."

She nodded toward a group of kids, among them Trevor and Chloe. Chloe was giggling and leaning against Trevor.

"She's touching him," said Emily. "Nothing is that funny that she needs to touch him."

"Maybe one of her ankles is bad and he's helping her stand," I said. "I mean, that would make *me* feel better."

Emily's ponytail whipped from side to side as she shook her head. "I saw her warming up earlier. She's in top form." Then, as an afterthought, she added, "Sorry."

"Well, I'm sure everything will be okay," I said. "If you want, I'll go check it out."

Emily's angry expression relaxed. "Would you?"

"Sure. And if one of her ankles isn't bad, I can change that," I said.

Emily stiffened and stared straight ahead. "As championship co-coordinator, I cannot approve of violence toward another player."

I rolled my eyes. "It was a joke. I won't lay a finger on her."

"If you do," Emily whispered, "make sure it's just to push her away from Trevor."

She resumed her wooden stance while I trotted over to my Champs classmates. Everyone greeted me, except Chloe of course, and went back to talking about their fund-raising and game strategy.

"So are you and your brothers ready?" asked Trevor, pulling me slightly to the side.

Chloe was talking to one of the other girls, but her eyes were on me.

"Oh, yeah," I said, waving my hand dismissively. "We've got the fire-making down and we've planned out how we'll approach almost any obstacle."

"That's good," said Trevor. "Chloe's been pretty much running the show for us, so as long as we do what she says, it'll be great!" He smiled, but his teeth barely showed.

"She's not much of a team player, is she?" I asked.

He dropped the happy act. "She is . . . if it's a team of one."

"That sounds like her," I said. "But at least you guys already know what you're up against."

"I don't think it'll matter," he said. "Ms. Success wouldn't let us be a team of two so we had to invite Shelly."

"Then you have an extra player to help you! That's . . ." I saw the sour look on his face. "That's *not* good?"

"Shelly practiced with us on Friday and Saturday." Trevor stepped closer and spoke in a low voice. "And I kept waiting for the mother ship to come and whisk her back to her home planet. She's a total space cadet."

"Why? She doesn't follow the leader?"

"Oh, she follows just fine," said Trevor. "When the leader's a butterfly or squirrel."

I wanted to laugh, but I knew Trevor was making jokes to cover up his disappointment.

"Sorry," I said again. I noticed Ms. Success stepping onto a tree stump, with her whistle and clipboard in hand. "I should probably get back to my brothers. Good luck in there."

"You too," said Trevor.

I hurried over to my family, giving Emily an encouraging nod. From the way Trevor talked, she didn't have anything to worry about.

Ms. Success blew a trill note on her whistle, and the Champs gathered around with their parents.

"Hello to all of you!" she boomed. "And welcome to the fifth-annual Champs Championship!"

The audience cheered and applauded.

"In just a moment, we'll be sending our first group into the obstacle course. There are ten obstacles, which I've personally run with my co-coordinator." She nodded at Emily.

"Therefore, I can tell you it's possible to make it through in thirty-five minutes or less."

"Ten obstacles, thirty-five minutes," whispered Parker. "Three and a half minutes per obstacle."

"There will be a course judge watching you at all times," she continued. "And because I care about the well-being of my students, we've got trained EMTs standing by to treat injuries." Ms. Success raised an eyebrow. "Real injuries, folks. Not boo-boos or owies." Then she called out the team positions and members. After she read off our team, she lowered her clipboard.

"Sadly, I can't allow any of you to watch the other teams run the course until you've done so yourself," she said. "But while you wait, I've set up a few shows for your viewing pleasure." She pointed to a film projector and a large white sheet tied to some trees to make a movie screen.

"What's the first show?" asked Nick.

Ms. Success tilted her head modestly. "A little something from my theater days. I was Eliza Doolittle in *My Fair Lady*."

"Oh." Nick smiled at her, then turned to us. "That combination of words means nothing to me."

"It's a musical," said Parker.

"Ugh," said Nick.

"So without further ado," continued Ms. Success, "let's send our first group onto the course!"

The audience cheered again and Team One headed for the starting line. As soon as they'd vanished into the forest, the crowd settled down to watch Ms. Success butcher a British accent.

About forty-five minutes into the show, Team One re-emerged, red-faced and sweating. One of them, Tan Dan, had scraped up his legs, and the entire team was wet and muddy.

"That doesn't look promising," said Parker.

"Maybe you should have brought a shower cap," said Nick.

A woman in an EMT uniform pulled Dan aside while his teammates went back down to watch the next group.

Ms. Success shook her head and pointed to the movie screen. "They're going to miss a quality dance number."

My brothers and I struggled through the show while four more teams disappeared into the forest. When Team Six got up to take their turn, Nick, Parker, and I stepped away from the film to warm-up.

"What's the fastest time for the course?" I asked.

"Thirty-six minutes," said Parker, consulting the clipboard Ms. Success had left out. "By . . . surprise, surprise . . . Chloe, Trevor, and Shelly."

"Darn," I said.

Chloe had turned out to be a better leader than I'd

hoped. My stomach started to fill with butterflies, and when Ms. Success called my name, I jumped with a start.

"Alexis, Nick and Parker!" called Ms. Success. "Team Seven is up."

My brothers and I looked at each other.

"Are we ready?" asked Parker, setting his watch.

Nick let out a deep breath and nodded. "Alex?"

I bent into a runner's lunge. "Thirty-five minutes or bust."

Chapter 16 ✤

G o!" shouted Ms. Success.

My brothers and I sprinted away from the starting line while Dad shouted words of encouragement after us. The forest opened up around us until the air was rich with the scent of pine and much cooler from the shade of the trees.

The first three obstacles were easy. We had to run through tires, cross some monkey bars, and climb a six-foot wall. Nick pretty much threw me and Parker over, and was able to shimmy up on his own.

"Ninety seconds down," said Parker as we raced for the fourth obstacle.

When we reached it, however, we came to a dead stop.

A wooden plank sat in the center of a huge circle of bricks. A thick mountain of rope was coiled up on the outside.

"I don't get it," I said. "What are we supposed to do?"

"Look!" Parker pointed to a sheet of paper nailed to a tree beside the circle. He slipped the paper off the nail and the three of us read:

> Retrieve the board for use in the next obstacle.
> No person can touch the ground inside the
> circle, and the circle can't be broken.

"Okay," said Parker, "so we'll just lasso the board and pull it out."

He put the note back and picked up the rope. After creating a loop in one end, he tossed the rope at the board and maneuvered himself around the circle, trying to slip the loop over the wood.

"That's not going to work," said Nick. "The board's flat against the ground and the rope's too thick." He glanced up at the tree. "Give it here."

Parker did as he was told, and Nick tossed the looped end of the rope over one of the tree's bigger branches. It came down on the other side and Nick held it out to me.

"Put this around your waist," he said, tying another loop on the opposite end.

"A rope-and-pulley system!" Parker smacked himself in the forehead. "Why didn't I think of that?"

I shimmied into the loop and Nick did the same on his end. Then, he started to back away, clutching the rope in front of him with both hands. I slowly started to lift off the ground, swinging back and forth.

"Parker, push her toward the center of the circle," grunted Nick, leaning back with all his weight and digging his heels into the ground. "Then come help me."

"I don't weigh *that* much!" I said, as Parker pointed me in the direction of the board and gave a hearty shove. I soared to the opposite end of the circle, but my fingers were inches away from the board.

"Lower me a bit," I said.

Even with Parker's help, I knew Nick was having trouble keeping my height steady and that there was a very real chance he'd drop me straight to the ground.

"Easy does it," grunted Parker, and I felt the rope slip a few inches.

I tried again and gripped the edge of the board with my fingers. Straining my entire arm, I pulled the board to a vertical position. Unfortunately, it was too heavy for me to throw outside the circle, and my momentum had stopped so I was stranded in the center.

"Use the board like an oar," called Nick. "Row yourself to the edge."

He made it sound way easier than it actually was. After what felt like a thousand lifetimes, I finally got close enough for Parker to take the board from me.

"Later, sucker!" he said as soon as he had it.

"Hey!"

"Just kidding." He tossed the board aside and took my hands. Looking back at Nick, he yelled, "Ready?"

Nick let the slack out of the rope at the same time Parker pulled me toward him with all his strength. We fell to the ground in an unceremonious heap, but my entire body avoided the inner circle.

"Good job, guys!" said Nick, running over to join us. "Parker, time?"

Parker winced at his watch. "We're at six minutes."

"Then we'd better get going." Nick slapped him on the shoulder and sprinted with the board under one arm toward the next obstacle.

Again, we came to a dead stop, this time at a pond. It was only about fifty feet across, but it was too deep to wade. Two rain barrels stood just beneath a tree with another note tacked to it. I picked it up and read, "Use the board and the barrels to cross the pond. Your upper body cannot touch the water."

I put down the note and studied the barrels, prying the lids off of them.

"Hey! Whoa!" both my brothers cried.

"*What?*" I fought to keep the exasperation out of my voice. "There's no other way to get into the barrels."

Nick goggled at me. "You want to ride *inside* them?"

"No, I want *you* guys to ride inside them. I'll balance on top of each one and roll it to the opposite shore." I stood on top of one and demonstrated. "I saw a lumberjack do it with a log once."

Parker rubbed his forehead. "There are several problems with that plan, the most obvious being that you are not a lumberjack."

"But I've got great balance," I said. "You've seen."

Parker stared at me in amazement. "It doesn't mean I want to climb inside a sealed container and let you push it to the center of a lake!"

"A *pond*," I corrected.

"I'm with Parker," said Nick. "We need to be on the outside of the barrels. . . . Maybe moving ourselves along with the plank?"

Parker chewed his lip and walked around the objects a few times. "I've got a better idea."

Following his instructions, we resealed the barrels and

tilted them on their sides, Parker climbing on one and I on the other. Then we propped the plank between them and sat on either end, while Nick rested his upper body on the plank's center. He kicked his feet in the water and steered our makeshift raft to the opposite shore.

"Time?" he asked.

"We're at twelve minutes," said Parker.

"We're barely keeping on time." Nick gritted his teeth. "The next ones had better be easy."

Thankfully, obstacle six was a rope climb with a platform at the top leading to obstacle seven. Although my legs still hurt from earlier that week, my brothers and I mastered the ropes in a minute flat. Once we reached the platform, Parker read the note taped to a pole beside it.

"To get to obstacle seven, cross the mud pit."

We all looked down at the long stretch of brown sludge that spread between us and the next obstacle.

"Nooo," said Parker.

"That explains the muddy kids," I said.

Nick pointed at the note. "There are two ways across. Traverse the mud, or solve the riddles and free the flying foxes."

"Augh!" Parker dropped the note and jumped back.

"What? What's going on?" Nick and I bumped into each other, twirling around to see what had startled Parker.

"Flying foxes!" he said. "Those furry demons have mastered flight?!"

Nick and I stopped moving and laughed.

"A flying fox isn't an animal," I said. "It's a little set of handlebars that run on . . . that."

I pointed to a cable above us, roughly thirty feet off the ground. It slanted down to a platform on the opposite side of the mud pit.

"Oh." Parker looked sheepish.

"And I'm guessing the foxes are in there." Nick pointed to a long box resting along the edge of the platform.

We stepped closer and saw three combination locks securing the box lid. Each lock had five rotating dials, but instead of numbers, the dials held letters.

I groaned. "There's got to be like a hundred possible combinations on each lock!"

"A hundred thousand," corrected Parker, inspecting the dials. "But there's also got to be a clue here somewhere." He lifted the box and pointed. "Ha!"

On the bottom were written three lines:

> *What should all Champs have?*
> *(Hint: A group of lions.)*
> *What should all Champs be?*
> *(Hint: The sun is one.)*

Instead of jumping into action, my brothers and I just stared at the box.

"I think we were better off *without* the clues," I said. "What do you call a group of lions?"

Nick shrugged. "Dangerous?"

I scratched my head. "So all Champs should be dangerous?"

"No," said Parker. "All Champs should be like the sun."

Nick stepped away to glance down at the mud. "Do you want to carry Parker, or should I?"

I joined him. "You're training to be his servant, right? I think this would be good practice."

"Maybe he can walk if we promise to keep his hair dry," said Nick.

Behind us, Parker, fiddled with the locks. "Not likely."

"Besides, how would we do that?" I asked. "*Did* you bring a shower cap?"

"No, but the Swiss Army knife might have one. It's got everything."

There was a loud thump behind us, and Nick and I glanced at Parker, who was grinning triumphantly.

"Shall we?" he asked, holding up a flying fox.

Nick and I stared open-mouthed at him.

"You did it!" I said. "How?"

Parker tapped his head. "I used my mental computer."

"Ohhh," said Nick and I.

"All Champs should use their *brains*," said Nick. "What were the other two?"

"A group of lions is a pride, and the sun is a . . ." He pointed to the star on his chest.

I applauded Parker, and Nick gave him a fist bump. "Nice one! I knew we kept you around for a reason."

Parker blushed and smiled even wider. "How does this thing work anyway?" He held the flying fox out and I took it, attaching it to the overhead wire.

"It works like *this*." I lifted my legs off the platform and tucked them in to my chest. The wire sagged a little under my weight, but the flying fox propelled me forward and down to the other platform. When I was steady on both feet again, I gave a thumbs-up and Parker soared down on his flying fox, followed by Nick.

"We're at nineteen minutes," said Parker before Nick could even ask. "The next obstacle takes us back to the ground."

He pointed to an enormous net that angled downward from the ledge of the platform to obstacle nine. "We'll have to carefully—"

"No, we won't," said Nick. Then folding his arms over his chest, he rolled off the ledge and all the way down the net, hitting the ground with a small cloud of dust. "Quick and *almost* painless," he called up, rubbing his backside.

"You heard the man," I said, giving Parker a gentle nudge. Unfortunately, I caught him off guard and he toppled face-first into the net, bouncing wildly all the way down.

"Augh . . . augh . . . augh!" he cried with each bounce.

"Sorry!" I shouted, sliding down after him.

Parker's nose was planted in the ground when I touched down, but he groaned and held up his watch arm.

"We've got fifteen minutes left," I said.

Nick and I helped Parker to his feet, and the three of us hurried over to a low crawl under a series of crisscrossing ropes. We all suffered a few cuts and bruises but made it to the other side in two minutes. We now had thirteen minutes left to tackle the final obstacle and make it back to the starting line.

But obstacle ten didn't look to be an easy task. It required running along a series of narrow beams that led to a springboard. On the other side of the board stood a six-foot padded platform that was wedged between two trees. From one of the tree's branches hung three gold stars.

Nick grabbed a note off a nearby tree. "Cross all the beams, make it to the top of the platform, and grab a star. If you fall off a beam, you must start over."

"Great," said Parker. "Who wants to unleash their inner gymnast first?"

"I'll go," I said.

"Take it slow," said Nick. "You don't want to get careless and fall off."

"Got it," I said. Then I turned and sprinted across the planks full speed.

"Alex!" he shouted.

But I ignored him. At my height and strength, if I was going to make it to the platform, I'd have to reach the springboard at a run. Since the beams were laying on the ground and hadn't been secured to anything, they wobbled a bit, but I expertly crossed three of them. The fourth shifted slightly in a direction that I didn't anticipate, and my foot slipped and hit the dirt.

"Darn it," I muttered.

"I told you!" said Nick.

"Let me try again!" I ran to the start and jumped onto the first beam. My brothers stood quietly behind me, as if any sound might knock me off balance. With just a few wobbly steps, I reached the edge of the final beam and jumped with both feet onto the springboard.

It had more bounce to it than I expected, and launched me high enough for my upper body to connect with the platform. I clung to it for dear life and pulled myself up. Once I was back on my feet, I grabbed one of the stars from the tree.

"Nothing to it!" I called to Nick and Parker.

And with those words, I jinxed my brothers.

Parker went next but kept falling off about halfway through.

"Try *not* running," said Nick.

"If Alex can do it, I can do it!" he panted.

After his fourth failed attempt, Parker *walked* the beams and turned to the obstacle course judge. "The note says I just have to get across the beams and onto the platform. It doesn't say how, right?"

"Correct," said the judge.

Parker stepped onto solid ground and, without so much as a glance at the springboard, shimmied up one of the trees beside the platform. He grabbed his own star from the tree branch and avoided my disapproving gaze.

"I prefer to blaze my own trail," he said with a haughty sniff.

Nick struggled to make it to the end of the beams. He was waving his arms madly and tipping back and forth. If we hadn't been under a time crunch, I would have laughed. Nick reached the last beam with eight minutes left. All he had to do now was get up to the platform.

Nick jumped onto the springboard with both feet, but since he weighed a significant amount more than me, it sank and only propelled him a foot or so into the air.

"That's no good," said Parker. "Go up one of the trees."

Nick just stared at him. "That's like asking a rhino to climb a ladder. It's not gonna happen."

"Run across the beams and *jump* onto the springboard," I suggested, and Nick directed his incredulous gaze at me. "No, okay, bad idea."

"How can you be so athletic and unable to do *this*?" Parker asked his twin.

"Oh, I'm *sorry*." Nick's words dripped with sarcasm. "You want me to leap tall buildings in a single bound?"

"Not tall buildings. A six-foot wall!" cried Parker. "Evel Knievel could do it with his eyes closed."

"Evel Knievel had a motorcycle!" Nick shot back. "And a—" He stopped short, his eyes wide with revelation, and spun to face the course judge. "Can I move the beams after everyone's across?"

The course judge smiled. "Yes, you can."

Before he'd even picked up the first beam, Parker and I knew exactly what Nick had in mind.

He was going to build a ramp.

"Brilliant!" cried Parker.

"Woohoo!" I cheered.

Nick moved like lightning to angle all four beams side by side, against the platform.

"Time?" he asked Parker.

"Five minutes."

Nick rubbed his hands together and backed up. "Ladies and gentlemen, prepare for takeoff."

He sprinted toward his makeshift ramp, running up the beams. But with nothing to hold them together, the pieces of wood started to shake. Just as Nick reached the top, one of the beams under his right foot separated from the others. Nick's right side lurched downward as he started to fall, the entire inside of his leg scraping the next beam over.

He screamed in pain and scrabbled against the remaining beams to reach the top.

"Help him!" Parker leapt forward and took hold of one of Nick's arms. I dug my fingers into the other and we pulled with all our might.

Nick flopped onto the platform and rolled onto one side, clutching his leg.

"Nick!" I dropped down next to him, but he turned away.

"I'm good," he said through clenched teeth. But when he pulled his hands off his leg, I could see an ugly, red abrasion that went from his thigh to his calf. "Time?" he croaked.

"We've got three minutes," said Parker. He licked his lips

and swallowed. "But we can take it slow, Nick. We don't have to win."

It was a big sacrifice for Parker to make, and my throat tightened as I nodded in agreement. "We can cross the finish line whenever you want."

Nick smiled at both of us. "Thanks, guys. But if we don't win, how can I afford my crutches?"

Parker and I laughed, and Nick reached up to grab his star. Then the three of us dangled our legs over the edge of the platform and dropped to the ground. When we emerged from the forest, it was to a cheering crowd . . . and a time of thirty-five minutes and fourteen seconds. After the first round, we were in the lead.

❀ Chapter 17

Of course, the competition wasn't over yet, but everyone knew it was between our team and Chloe's.

"You're doing great!" said Dad, hugging the three of us and being extra careful with Nick. While he and my brothers went to have an EMT check Nick's leg, I wandered over to Emily. She was chewing on a fingernail and staring into space, a frown causing her forehead to wrinkle.

"What do you think?" I asked, holding my arms open. "Not too bad for an Energetic Evins."

Emily pulled herself back to the present and nodded.

"Come on," I nudged her. "You can't break your vow

of silence for a congratulations? Are you upset because we might beat Trevor?"

Emily turned her face toward the sun before meeting my eyes. "Alexis, I got a phone call about ten minutes ago. From your mom."

My heart pounded as fast as it had in the obstacle course. "What? She . . . she called back? Did you talk to her?"

Emily shook her head. "I thought about it, but let it go to voice mail." She held out her cell phone. "Do you want to hear it?"

I flinched as if she were offering me a writhing snake. The message I'd left Mom had been less than friendly. I doubted she had any kind words for me.

"The message isn't *that* bad," said Emily.

I raised my eyebrow, and she sighed. "Yes, I listened to it, okay? I only have so much self-control."

Without waiting for me to answer, Emily punched in the password for her voice mail and handed the phone to me. I hesitated before putting it to my ear.

". . . it's Mother. How are you." Mom's voice had the same no-nonsense tone as always. "I was surprised to hear from you, and a little taken aback by the harshness of your words." She paused. "Although I admit your anger may not be *entirely* unfounded. Please return my call so we can address our predicament."

Then she hung up.

I kept the phone to my ear, listening to make sure there weren't any other voice mails. There weren't.

"Well?" prompted Emily.

"She's the same old scientist," I said, handing Emily her phone. "And I'm just a problem to solve."

My words sounded more bitter than I expected, and I wondered if my brothers' loathing for Mom had started to influence me.

"What are you going to do?" asked Emily.

Several conflicting answers fought to reach my lips, but the only sound that came out was a frustrated grunt.

"I don't know," I shook my head. "I'll have to think about it."

Emily nodded, and I noticed that this time she didn't try to influence me. I could have hugged her.

"Well, my stepmom needs me to set up the third film so I should go," said Emily. She smiled at me. "Good luck in the next round."

"Thanks." I smiled back.

I scanned the crowd for my brothers, but unfortunately, Chloe found me first.

"It looks like we're pretty evenly matched," she said.

"Yep!" I couldn't resist a smug grin. "How's that for a little friendly competition?"

Chloe's face darkened. "I don't like it."

I sighed. "Of course you don't. I guess you'll just have to try harder at fire-making."

"Maybe," she said in a soft, creepy voice. "But that's not a guarantee, is it?"

I narrowed my eyes in suspicion. "What do you mean?"

Chloe held up her cell phone, pressed a few buttons, and a second later I heard my voice coming from the speaker.

". . . Emily's such a drama queen that she doesn't see it that way. It's always about her and how things affect *her*."

A chill went up my spine as I recalled the conversation. I'd had it with my brothers after Emily had gotten mad at me over Trevor.

Chloe leaned close. "That's Emily you're talking about, isn't it?"

The recording continued as I went down my laundry list of Emily's flaws, and I felt my cheeks getting warmer and warmer. Chloe stopped the recording and put her phone away.

"You know what would be so sad?" She pouted her lower lip. "If Emily found out what her dearest friend thought of her."

I shook my head. "I was just mad. . . ."

"You know what would be sadder?" continued Chloe. "If Emily knew that the same friend had to be paid just to hang out with her."

Chloe meant, of course, the twenty bucks she'd given me at the slumber party. I stared at her, feeling the fury build inside me. I'd always known the girl was evil, but up until now, I'd never known the true extent of it.

"What do you want?" I asked, my voice shaking with anger.

"I want you to throw the fire-making challenge," said Chloe.

"What?!" I cried.

"I'm *this* close to winning Trevor over," she said, holding her thumb and forefinger an inch apart. "If we take this competition, that's a thousand dollars he and I will have to spend together."

"With *Shelly*," I said.

Chloe rolled her eyes. "I could give that fool a stack of Champs change and she'd leave happy."

"Well, forget it," I said, turning to walk away.

"You're Emily's only true friend," Chloe said to my back. "Can you really hurt her like this?"

I stopped and stared at the ground. Emily had cared about me so much that she'd tracked down my mom. As far as I knew, she'd never said a harsh thing against me, and she'd certainly never paid anyone to hang out with me.

I *was* her only true friend. And she was one of mine. But she wouldn't be for long if she knew the truth.

I could hear Chloe breathing in my ear.

"You don't even have to do much," she said. "Just play dumb, and if your brothers get the fire going too soon, maybe kick a little dirt on it. That's all. And if you don't get a fire going *period*, you won't even have to feel guilty."

I stared straight ahead. "And you won't say anything to Emily?"

"Never, ever, ever," she promised.

When I didn't respond right away, she gave me one last thing to think about.

"Your brothers will forgive you if you don't win," she said. "Do you think Emily will forgive you if you do?"

A harsh tweeting sound filled the air, and we glanced over to where Ms. Success was rounding everyone up. Without another word to Chloe, I hurried over to join my family.

"Ladies and gentlemen!" bellowed Ms. Success. "We've had a wonderful first round of competition, with Teams Seven and Four in the lead."

Nick, Parker, and Dad cheered, but all I could muster was a weak clap.

"But it's our next round that will determine the champions of the Champs Championship!"

"Try saying *that* ten times fast," Parker whispered to me. I forced a smile.

"We've got a designated fire area, so as I call the teams, you'll follow me to the site and get . . . fired up!" She punched the air with her fist, and the crowd cheered. "Team One, bring the heat!"

"I hope we don't have to watch that movie again while we wait," Nick said in a low voice as the crowd dispersed.

"Nope. Looks like they're loading up a different film reel," said Parker.

I smiled as convincingly as I could. "Let's go see what's playing."

"There's not a sequel to *My Fair Lady*, is there?" asked Nick, following me.

"No," I said.

"Good."

As it turned out, the only thing worse than Ms. Success faking a British accent was Ms. Success faking multiple British accents. And that was what she did for the next film, her one-woman version of *Peter Pan*.

Thankfully, the fire-making took people a lot less time than the obstacle course did, and after only two hours, my brothers and I were up.

Ms. Success led us to a forest clearing marked by a charred spot on the ground. She gestured to a stack of firewood.

"All you have to do is keep a flame going long enough to break this string," she said, pointing to a piece of twine tied between two posts a foot above the charred spot.

She pulled a stopwatch out of her pocket and lifted it so we could read the zeroes. "And . . . begin."

Parker and Nick dashed around, searching for twigs and grabbing the firewood. I just stood there, kicking at the dirt. If Ms. Success thought it was strange, she didn't say anything. She did, however, glance up sharply when Nick said a curse word.

"We've got plenty of wood but nothing to use as tinder!" he said. "The other teams must have taken it all."

Parker groaned and ran a hand through his hair. "There's got to be something. Can we burn our shirts?"

Ms. Success cleared her throat loudly, and Parker jumped.

"I mean, uh, it'd be a tragedy, but if we had to—"

Nick shook his head. "They'd catch fire almost as slowly as the wood."

I continued to stand off to the side by myself, arms crossed, watching my brothers struggle and feeling about two inches tall.

"We can burn leaves," said Parker, pointing up. "We just have to get them out of the trees."

"If that's the best we can do," said Nick. "I'll search some more for twigs. You and Alex get the leaves." For the first time, he noticed my silence. "Okay, Alex? We need your help."

But I couldn't. Not if I wanted to save Emily from my betrayal.

"I . . . I . . ." I shook my head and tears filled my eyes.

Nick put a hand on my arm. "What's wrong?"

"Are you sick?" asked Parker, joining us. "Do you need a doctor?"

Both of my brothers looked so concerned that my tears spilled over even more and splattered in the dirt. Ms. Success was watching me too, so Nick and Parker pulled me out of earshot.

And then I blurted everything about Emily, and Chloe, and Trevor. When I stopped confessing, I realized that all three of us were now sitting, Nick chewing on his knuckles and Parker massaging his scalp between his hands.

"Do you hate me?" I asked, sniffling and wiping my eyes.

Parker stopped rubbing. "Well, on a scale of one to ten . . ."

Nick elbowed him. "No, we don't hate you. We're your brothers. But we're sad that you'd try to trick us."

Parker nodded, and I burst into fresh tears.

"I'm so, so sorry!" I threw my arms around Nick and then Parker. "I'm the worst person in the world!"

"Don't be silly," said Parker as I left huge tearstains on

his shirt. "Although you may be the *soggiest* person in the world."

I choked out a laugh and tried to compose myself.

"So what are we going to do?" asked Nick. "Do we take our sweet time so Chloe wins, or do we try and sweep this thing?"

I wrinkled my forehead. "Wait. You'd let us lose?"

Nick smiled sadly and shrugged. "If it means that much to you."

"Woah!" cried Parker. "I totally don't agree with that. I want a thousand dollars."

Nick gave him a look. "Even if it means Alex loses a friend?"

"She can buy a new one with her share of the money," said Parker. "And Emily isn't a very good friend to begin with if she'd dump Alex for making a few mistakes."

Nick opened his mouth to argue, but I stopped him.

"He's right. If I'm lucky, Emily will forgive me." I squeezed Nick's hand. "But I'm not going to let you guys down."

Nick squeezed back.

"Of course, it may not end up mattering," I said, inspecting the forest around us. "Without tinder, we don't have a chance. We need something flammable. . . . And lots of it."

And that was when my eyes fell on Parker.

I gasped and clapped a hand over my mouth, pointing at his hair.

"What?" he cried, covering his head. "Is it a flying fox?"

"No, your . . . your hair!" I sputtered. "It makes the perfect tinder!"

He backed away from me. "What?"

Nick's eyes lit up. "She's right! You have so much product in there that the alcohol alone would get this thing blazing!"

"You want me to cut off my hair?!" he shouted incredulously.

"It's for a good cause," I said. "Don't you want to win a thousand dollars?"

"Not like this!" Parker patted his hair protectively.

"Your hair will grow back, Parker," said Nick. "But this is a one-time chance for a *lot* of money."

"But what would I spend it on?" whimpered Parker. "I won't need any more hair products if I'm bald!"

"We've been through a lot together, and we've sacrificed so much!" I said. "I'm about to lose one of the few friends I have; Nick tore up his leg. . . . Won't you take one for the team?"

Parker was quiet, and I could feel the seconds trickling away. Finally, he handed over his Swiss Army knife, the scissors jutting out.

Nick clapped him on the shoulder, and I hugged him.

The expression on Ms. Success's face was priceless as she watched us playing barber on Parker instead of building a fire. Parker kept his eyes closed the whole time, refusing to watch his lovely locks leave him.

When we felt confident we had enough, Nick struck the flint over it, and sparks settled into the hair, starting a small blaze.

"It worked!" I cried.

"It smells," said Parker, wrinkling his nose.

"Bring the twigs," said Nick. "We need to keep the blaze going."

From the sidelines, I heard a "Huh!" and looked up to see Ms. Success shaking her head in amazement.

We stoked the fire, coaxed the fire, and practically sang to the fire, until the string finally snapped.

And while Ms. Success told us our time wasn't the best, it was enough to squeeze past Chloe's team for first place.

"Yes!" shouted Nick, punching the air.

Parker and I hugged and jumped up and down. I even allowed myself one tiny squeal.

When we rejoined the crowd, the expressions on our faces said everything. Dad bear-hugged us each in turn, and Emily and Trevor ran over, followed closely by Chloe. Her eyes were burning holes through me, and I knew there was no stopping her.

So I confessed to Emily before she could.

"Emily," I said, taking her hand, "when you got mad at me the other day, I said some mean things about you to make myself feel better."

She blinked and frowned. "Okay."

"And when we were first becoming friends, I had Chloe pay me twenty dollars to keep you entertained at her party."

Emily's frown deepened. "You . . . you needed money to hang out with me?" Beside her, Chloe smirked and crossed her arms.

"I'm sorry," I told Emily. "I know what I did was wrong, but I'm new to this friendship thing. I mean, you're my first real friend. I don't want to lose you. And if you can ever forgive me, I promise I'll try harder."

Emily's entire face scrunched up and her fists clenched at her sides, but instead of yelling, she reached out and hugged me. "Oh, Alexis! Of course I forgive you!"

"Oof!" was all I could reply as she squeezed the air out of me.

"You've got to be kidding." Chloe grunted in disgust.

I glared at her. "Don't you have somewhere to be?"

Chloe narrowed her eyes. "Oh, suddenly you're the tough girl again?"

"I've always been the tough girl," I told her. "It doesn't mean I can't have weak moments."

Emily put an arm around me. "And when they happen, she has friends who can be tough *for* her."

Chloe backed off, shaking her head. "Whatever. You deserve each other."

"Yeah." I smiled at Emily. "We definitely do."

No sooner had Chloe stepped away than someone shoved in to fill her place in the crowd.

"Parker!" cried a pretty brunette girl. Her eyes were wide and she was taking in the former glory of his hair. "Parker, what happened?"

"Ashley?" my brother, pink-cheeked but pleased, pushed his way toward her. "What are you doing here?"

Ashley pointed to Nick. "Your brother told me . . ." She reached out to Parker and touched a short patch of hair. "How did this happen?"

Parker put his hand on hers. "We needed something to start the fire with." He shrugged and grinned sheepishly. "And it's only hair."

With a dramatic gasp and a lower lip quiver, Ashley threw her arms around Parker and kissed him.

"Aw," said Emily.

"Ew," said Nick and I.

A half hour later, Ms. Success presented my brothers and me with our championship check. We waved to the cheering crowd while Dad, beaming proudly, stood behind us.

As I felt the strength and comfort of my family's presence, I realized that I'd been handling the situation with Mom all wrong. I'd accused Emily of being self-absorbed, but when it came to my long-lost parent, I acted as if my attempts to reconnect with her only affected *me*. I couldn't ignore the feelings of my brothers or Dad anymore. Whatever problems we faced, we had to face them as a family.

Later, when the crowd dispersed and we were walking back to the car, I grabbed Dad's hand in one of mine and faced my brothers.

"What's up, Alex?" asked Nick.

After a deep, calming breath, I looked each member of my family in the eye. "We need to have another talk about Mom."